. . . Their lips met. Just lightly. Innocently. But then they lingered a few seconds, past innocence. "Congratulations again," Maggie said. "Good night." Then the slam of the car door.

Natalie waited until Maggie's car started before she pulled out into the street. She was stunned and embarrassed by her reaction to the kiss. She reached her hand to her lips. Thought of Maggie's lips: soft, slightly open. She couldn't read the kiss; she'd had wine, Maggie had had wine. Probably nothing to it. A kiss like that after an evening like theirs probably signified as much as a warm handshake after you haven't seen someone in a long time. She reminded herself that she was almost forty years old. That Maggie was only twenty-four. Natalie felt stirrings of an excitement she hadn't experienced since she first met Annie.

About the Author

Elisabeth Nonas was born in New York City in 1949. In 1977 she moved to Los Angeles, where she lives with her lover. She currently teaches fiction writing at UCLA Extension and is working on her third novel.

A Room Full of Women

Elisabeth Nonas

The Naiad Press, Inc.
1990

Printed in the United States of America
First Edition

Edited by Katherine V. Forrest
Cover design by Pat Tong and Bonnie Liss
    (Phoenix Graphics)
Typeset by Sandi Stancil

Library of Congress Cataloging-in-Publication Data

Nonas, Elisabeth, 1949—
    A room full of women / by Elisabeth Nonas.
        p.   cm.
    ISBN 0-941483-69-X
    I. Title.
PS3564.045R66   1990
813'.54--dc20
                                                                90-6131
                                                                CIP

Again —
and always —
for Carole

Acknowledgements

I would like to thank the following people for explaining to me what it is they do, and for providing me with technical advice about their various fields: Diane Abbitt; Roberta Bennett; Joyce Ellis; Susan Healy; Bee Ottinger; Joanne Steuer.

Thanks also to Pat Eliet for her encouragement, comments and advice throughout the various stages of this book.

And finally, I want to thank Katherine Forrest for her insightful and perceptive editing, as well as her generous support.

Chapter One
Cut to the Chase

"Don't follow me unless you mean it, honey."

Blair smiled, looked into her rear view mirror again. The white Mustang convertible had been behind her for miles, almost since she'd left her office in Hollywood and headed out Sunset Boulevard towards the beach. Blair guessed the woman at the wheel to be in her late twenties. She had short curly dark hair, wore Ray Bans, and had a very powerful car stereo that Blair could hear when they stopped for a light. From the volume of the music, Blair surmised the woman liked Annie Lennox. A lot. That was all the information she could gather from her vantage point, but she was so used to sizing up women that she automatically imagined the kind of body this one would have.

The woman pulled her car up alongside Blair's TR-6 at the next light. Pushing her Ray Bans onto her forehead, she squinted against the late afternoon sun. "What year is it?" she nodded towards the Triumph.

"Seventy-one."

"It's in great shape."

"Thanks." Blair had bought it the day after her mother disowned her. Tess, her lover at the time, had taken her to the car lot mostly to get her out of the house. They hadn't had any intention of driving off with a car, much less a used one, but Blair had fallen in love with the bright red TR-6. To this day, Tess maintained that red was the only color that could have penetrated the cloud of rage and pain surrounding Blair.

The light changed. As Blair drove away, the white car was stuck behind a stalled truck. Blair caught a glimpse of the Mustang's plates: R.M.T. Who was following her? Rose? Robin? Rachel?'

Traffic was moderately heavy, the road winding, so Blair concentrated on her driving. But she kept an eye on her rear view mirror, suspecting that she hadn't seen the last of R.M.T. She was no stranger to such pursuits; women had always followed her.

As she often did when she had a problem to solve, she'd left the office early and taken the long way home. Her project for this evening was a re-design on

2

the labels for a line of Mexican foods. The ad agency handling *¡Sabroso!* wanted to capitalize on the current vogue for hot and spicy dishes. Blair already had a few thoughts and would put them into thumbnails — small sketches of her ideas — when she got home. She also wanted to review her notes for a presentation she had to give later in the week, on a new line of microwave frozen dinners from Dinnertime, one of Kaplan/Shaw's biggest accounts. This detour had always been her way to relax, clear her head of petty office politics and problems so she could concentrate on what really needed to be accomplished. But she found it hard to keep her mind on work today.

The road wound through Beverly Hills and Bel Air. Just as Blair was passing UCLA, the white car reappeared, cutting in and out of traffic, speeding closer until it was behind her again. And there it stayed.

They snaked through Brentwood. The distant hills, the architecturally interesting houses, all Blair's usual distractions, didn't interest her today, had been replaced by R.M.T. Sometimes Blair lost sight of her companion around the winding curves. Blair wondered if she — Rhonda? Randi? Rebecca? — had turned onto a cross street, thus ending their little game. But then the Mustang always reappeared.

Coming to an intersection just as a light turned yellow, Blair gave an extra kick to the gas pedal and sped through. Looking back, she saw the Mustang accelerate to keep up with her. She smiled to herself.

In Pacific Palisades, she checked her mirror again. Okay, R.M.T., let's see how serious you are. She cut abruptly into a gas station. Caught by surprise, the

Mustang went past the first driveway before screeching up the next, backing, and then pulling around to the other side of the pump Blair was using.

The women smiled at each other as they stepped out of their cars. Blair had guessed right. The other woman had a nice body: athletic, but not thin. At about five feet-four, she was five inches shorter than Blair, a little overweight, but sturdily so. She wore electric-blue lycra running tights and a baggy, thick cotton pullover. She was probably closer to thirty-five — Blair's own age — than Blair had guessed earlier.

The woman had taken the cap off her gas tank, but was having trouble fitting the nozzle into it. She smiled sheepishly at Blair. She had managed to get herself tangled in the thick rubber hose in such a way that she couldn't move in any direction, couldn't release the hose to put it back on the pump or bring it forward to her car.

Before Blair could do anything to help, a gas station attendant hurried over. He untangled the woman and hooked the nozzle into the tank. Then he stood looking at both cars, and their drivers. "Beautiful cars, beautiful women," he said in a Middle-Eastern accent. "You are friends?"

The other woman answered him without taking her eyes from Blair: "Not yet." Blair smiled. She had wondered who would make the first move, and now the attendant had taken care of that for her. She walked over to the other woman, extending her hand. "I'm Blair Wilder."

The woman took Blair's hand. "Roxanne Tucker."

"Do you live out here?" Blair asked.

"No. Santa Monica."

"Then we're almost neighbors," Blair said. "I live in Venice."

"Isn't this a long way home?" Roxanne asked.

Blair shrugged. "I like the ride. What about you?"

The woman looked at Blair. "Can't you tell?"

Blair could always tell, but didn't say this to Roxanne.

Customers were lining up waiting for the pumps. Hurriedly exchanging phone numbers, Blair and Roxanne agreed to meet for a drink sometime over the weekend. Then they got back into their cars and drove off, Roxanne heading back the way they'd come, Blair continuing west.

The air was heavily scented with citrus and pungent eucalyptus. Neon signs hissed on, sharp against the dusky sky still lit by the sun which had almost set. Blair drove through the mysterious light. She turned down Temescal Canyon Road towards the Pacific Coast Highway. The ocean came into view, looking like a wall set between the two slopes of the canyon.

She eased the car into its parking spot. She stopped in the lobby for her mail — all junk, plus a few magazines — then walked up the outside stairs to her apartment.

Her building, like all the others along the beach in Venice, was laid out to take maximum advantage of its site. Almost every room had a view because each unit was actually one long room arbitrarily divided by built-in counters or steps into a kitchen and a dining area and a high-ceilinged living room. Blair's bedroom was a loft overlooking the living room, and shared the view out of the floor-to-ceiling front windows. The second bedroom was the only room that didn't front the ocean. Its windows were high up in the wall, allowing air and a little light, but acknowledging that there wasn't anything worth seeing if you didn't face the beach. She had converted this room into her studio, with a drafting table and proper lighting, but she rarely used it, preferring to take her sketch pads and pencils or markers and sit in the living room or out on the terrace.

She dumped her portfolio on the couch and stepped outside. This was part of her evening ritual.

And it was because of this that she couldn't give up the condo. She was forever talking about buying in a more sane neighborhood, where she could have a yard, maybe, and a little privacy, definitely. Some place that wouldn't be overrun on the weekends. But she never did anything about it. She'd once gotten as far as making an offer on a small house in the Hollywood Hills. An ideal fixer-upper, her real estate agent called it. And it would have been perfect, with a guest house she could convert into a studio. But when the owner came back with an unreasonable counter, Blair had felt a tremendous sense of relief that the deal had fallen through. She couldn't give up Venice Beach any more than she could get rid of her car.

During the day a unique mix of types peopled Ocean Front Walk, but now the strand was cleared of all but the locals and a few late stragglers. A briny draft blew in off the water. Time hung in the air and everything looked calm — the wide expanse of sand,

6

the palms stirred by a light breeze, the even waves. Blair took strength from this golden hour.

She went upstairs to change her clothes. If she hurried, she could get in a short run before it was completely dark. She was just starting her stretches when the phone rang.

"Hi, is this Blair?"

"Yes."

"This is Roxanne. From the gas station."

As if Blair had forgotten. "Hi."

"Hi." Roxanne continued nervously, "I was wondering, the weekend seemed kind of far away. Maybe we could get together sooner?"

"What'd you have in mind?"

"Are you free tonight?"

"I brought work home . . ."

"It doesn't have to be dinner. We could just have a drink later."

Blair thought for a moment. She could get her run in, do a few concepts. What the hell. It would be nice to have something to look forward to. "Sure," she said.

Roxanne suggested a Tex-Mex restaurant up the coast known for its margaritas. Blair said she'd meet her there around nine-thirty.

She finished her stretches and went for her run. Her momentary guilt pangs at not leaving enough time for work had been replaced by a pleasant sense of anticipation.

Her friends often teased her about the image she felt she had to uphold, that of the swashbuckling heartbreaker. She was always dating, sometimes several women at the same time. Her friends wanted to know how she did it. They envied her her

7

conquests. So they said. But Blair sensed that the envy was mixed with pity, an attitude of "I'd rather have what I've got, even if it isn't as glamorous as what you've got."

What was so glamorous about being concerned about AIDS, needing to know her dates hadn't slept with anyone at risk in the past ten years? But Blair knew there was no point in arguing. Her friends treated her much the same way married clients coming to her office treated Larry, a single man. The guys would go up to him, give him a sly wink, a nudge in the ribs, "What I wouldn't give to be in your position again!"

She knew those clients and her friends were talking about some dream of freedom, some carefree time in their past. No one thought to envy her her moments alone: waking in the dark after a nightmare, always coming home to an empty apartment, worrying about what to do over the holidays. Such moments probably never occurred to them. Few married people acknowledged that they were glad to be out of the game because of AIDS and herpes and other sexually transmitted diseases. But she accepted all aspects and consequences of her life — and didn't want it any other way.

"But are you really happy?" her friend Leah was always asking her. Blair could truthfully answer yes. What most people called happiness, she didn't believe in. Bliss will turn on you every time, she was always warning Leah. Leah who chased her dream in every woman she met, never realizing it was the dream and not the woman she was in love with.

Blair had given up on those kinds of dreams. After a certain amount of time, and it varied from relationship to relationship, her lovers started eating away at her independence. Or tried to. She wouldn't stand for that. There were times, of course, when someone touched her or looked at her a certain way, and Blair could hear an echo in the center of her happy solitude. Just a little ding, indicating a hollowness that no amount of casual sex or string of lovers could muffle. But would marrying someone cover that? She thought not.

She ended her run with a sprint, then walked slowly back home, where she worked on her ideas for the re-design. Thinking about food made her hungry. A quick rummage through her refrigerator yielded nothing interesting, so she stuck a potato in the microwave. Six minutes later she dotted it with butter, and was resigned to a rather bland dinner when she figured, what the hell, and opened her sample jar of *¡Sabroso!* hot salsa and dumped some on her potato.

At eight-forty-five she took a shower. By nine-fifteen she was ready to go. She flipped on her answering machine before leaving the house, and extended the hours on the light timers, just in case she didn't get home until very late that night. Or very early the next morning.

Roxanne was waiting at the bar. She wore tight black jeans, red and black cowboy boots, and an oversized white shirt with a bolo tie. Her curly dark hair, which had blown freely in the car, was now moussed into slick, wet-looking curls.

Roxanne was a set decorator who had worked in

film and television. Now she did only commercials. "The money's better and the gigs are shorter," she explained. "When I went on location with a film, I'd be gone for months. Three weeks is a long time for a commercial. I've got a short attention span. When it comes to some things," she added slyly.

They had common ground in advertising, even knew some of the same people. Each talked about her side of the business. Their real communication, however, was carried on in looks and gestures, a hand lingering on an arm, knees touching under the table. Around eleven, Blair reluctantly said she had to be going.

They stood facing each other in the parking lot.

"Sure you don't want to come back with me?" Roxanne asked again.

"Another night," Blair said. Then: "You remind me of someone." She hadn't been aware until she'd said it.

"A ghost from your past?"

"No, nothing like that," Blair said.

But it was exactly like that. Exactly.

A full moon, yellow and enormous. The light it threw entered her bedroom as she and Hallie thrashed on the bed, grappling for possession of each other. Something dangerous was in the air that night, in the color of the moon. As Blair moved to lie between Hallie's legs, Hallie pulled back, held her at arm's length. "Please, just for tonight, because of the moon, tell me you love me. Blair . . . Please."

For the rest of the week, Blair was too busy with

work to spend any conscious time thinking about how much Roxanne reminded her of Hallie. At odd, unguarded moments — just before sleep, or when engrossed in drawing, or when coming out of a meeting — short clips from her last years in San Francisco would flicker in her mind. The hospital, relief with Hallie and later, other women. An odd mix of specific moments — a nurse adjusting her father's pillow, the doctor patiently listening to a dream her father had — and a general sense of atmosphere: huge sky and clouds after rain, too hot for the raincoat she'd put on in the morning. Almost subliminal, the memories were impossible to defend against.

"Blair . . . Please."

Blair adjusted the silver lamé headband before stepping back to get the full effect of her costume. She had concocted a space age outfit from a pair of black leather pants and a white silk top with padded shoulders, using foaming mousse that added washable color to paint turquoise highlights in her light brown hair. The color made her pale grey eyes almost blue. The silver headband was the finishing touch. She wasn't much for costumes, but everyone seemed to get into the spirit of Halloween for Annie and Natalie's party. Women who ordinarily wouldn't be caught dead out of their tailored slacks or jeans planned their costumes months in advance, some as early as the moment they left the previous year's party.

Annie and Natalie's Halloween event — for it

11

seemed bigger than a party — had become a tradition among their friends. In the fourth year, the guest list had grown from forty to about seventy women. When a couple broke up, the next year each woman would be invited with her new lover, and she'd maybe bring a friend or two. Annie and Natalie had threatened that this was going to be their last Halloween party, their house simply wasn't big enough to accommodate all the marriages and divorces in the community.

Leah maintained that there wouldn't be so many breakups if more relationships were like Annie and Natalie's. Together forever, they had even publicly declared it in a commitment ceremony on their fifth anniversary. Together ten years, they had established themselves as a steady commodity in an unsteady community.

Blair believed they were the exception rather than the rule. She believed that women liked to marry. Instead of going out with several different people, they glommed onto one person for a time, participating in a kind of serial monogamy. Like Leah, they wanted marriage, a house and a white picket fence and a theme song. Just like straight America. Blair didn't buy the dream. Without the responsibilities of straight America, namely children, why should they be constrained by straight America's idea of relationships?

"It doesn't have anything to do with gay or straight," Leah argued with her. "Besides, you wouldn't think that if you weren't so gorgeous."

"What does that have to do with anything?"

"It makes it much easier for you."

Blair couldn't judge, but many people told her she was beautiful. She knew people looked at her. She once tried to attribute this attention to her height. "They don't stare because you're five-nine," Tess told her. "Face it, you're movie star beautiful." Often, when she was at the movies or a concert, someone would approach her and ask timidly, "Are you someone?" Her beauty was intimidating to some people, she knew, and attractive to others.

Blair had to park several houses past Annie and Natalie's. Because of the way noise carried in the canyons, she could hear the party as she walked down the hill. She felt a familiar excitement in the pit of her stomach. Each party was a challenge to her: she eagerly anticipated something, or someone, waiting for her. A vampire and werewolf, capes billowing, strode up the driveway ahead of her. More cars arrived as she stepped onto the patio.

The back of the house opened onto the patio and pool deck. Pumpkins, candles flickering through scraggly grins and grimaces, had been placed at intervals around the pool. It was like walking onto a model of a house split open to reveal its interior. Blair could see the entire scene set before her. The party had spilled outside from the living room, and women in all sorts of costumes wandered about or stood talking in small groups. At one poolside table a pirate and a doctor carried on a heated discussion about an openly gay political candidate. Two little leaguers chatted with a Viking and a cowboy. Looking inside, Blair saw Annie take the capes of the vampire and werewolf, then disappear into another room.

Someone meowed behind her, and she turned

around to see a perfect, though human-sized and upright, cat.

"What do you think?" the feline asked.

Blair peered into the elaborately made-up face. "Tess?"

"How'd you know?" Tess sounded disappointed.

"I'd recognize that meow anywhere." Not to mention the already obvious smell of liquor on her breath. Tess must have started early this evening.

Tess turned around slowly to give Blair the full effect of the costume. "I rented it at a wardrobe house."

"It's terrific." Blair admired the details. Tess had painted whiskers on her face, and a black button nose.

"I've been practicing keeping my fingers curled into paws." Tess waved a chubby mitt and moved on to say hello to someone else.

Blair made her way inside, picking up a beer as she passed the bar. A marine and a Gypsy huddled nearby, exchanging the latest gossip on which TV stars were gay.

Natalie Bazarian was the perfect hostess. Every time Blair saw her she was either bringing someone something to drink or complimenting a guest on her costume.

This year Natalie was dressed as a hippy, barefoot, with peace patches sewn all over her cut-off jeans. She wore several strands of beads which she showed off by keeping her workshirt, festooned with buttons from student protest days, open practically to her navel. More than one guest, tortilla chip in hand, missed the dip when Natalie walked by.

Blair was surprised at how natural Natalie looked

in her outfit, much more so than her usual work uniform, when she dressed the part of the successful real estate attorney.

Natalie was a big woman. Tall and self-assured, a definite presence. Her hair, thick and shiny black, with a wave of grey sweeping off her right temple, gave her a rather dashing look. Thick straight brows over brown eyes flecked with gold, nose a little too big, and a sensuous mouth. Everything worked together and her face was very handsome.

Annie was attractive in a more quiet way, her presence womanly and calm. She had a softness that was immediately appealing. Tonight she had pulled her light brown shoulder-length hair back off her face, and poured herself into tight Levis and black boots. A pack of cigarettes rolled into one sleeve of her white T-shirt completed the Fifties hood uniform.

Despite the get-up, there was no way Annie Weiss could look tough. Her clothes only emphasized her thin body; her pulled back hair accented her high cheekbones and delicate mouth. She appeared innocent and vulnerable. "Love your tattoos," Blair commented as she kissed Annie's cheek.

"Natalie did them all. This one's my favorite." On Annie's biceps a hula girl danced on a scroll reading "Natalie."

Natalie joined them. "And you thought you had no competition in the drawing department," she said, hugging Blair. "Hard to believe we're all responsible adults, isn't it?" She gestured towards the room. "I just love this party. Look at Shirley, dressed as Dudley Do-Right." Natalie was grinning broadly. "Uhp, I think Tess found someone."

Blair scanned the room. Tess wasn't hard to find.

Her cat outfit had ears and a three-foot tail. Also, she was talking to a woman who had come in a very elaborate Big Bird costume. They were trying to find a way for Big Bird to sit down.

Natalie surveyed the room again. "I wish people would start dancing." She grabbed Leah who was just walking by. "Come on, Lachman, dance with me."

"It's a little early for that," Leah protested.

Annie put her hand on Natalie's arm. "Honey, don't make Leah dance if she doesn't want to."

"But this is a party. *You* dance with me, then. That'll get everyone started." Natalie grabbed Annie, spun her around once.

Annie held Natalie still. "When they want to dance, they'll dance. Don't worry. What are you drinking?"

"Am I being obnoxious?"

"Verging. Maybe it's time for seltzer."

"It's not like she's got to drive home," Blair interceded on Natalie's behalf.

"Nah, it's okay. I'll take a break," Natalie said, kissing Annie on the cheek. "I love you." She looked at Blair and Leah. "I love you guys, too, but differently."

Annie watched Natalie saunter off. "Don't encourage her, Blair."

"I think she's cute." Blair had never seen her friend really drunk, and rather enjoyed the looser Natalie, though she wouldn't say as much to Annie.

Annie hadn't taken her eyes off Natalie. Blair followed her gaze, and saw Natalie loading a plate with food. "Don't worry about her," Blair reassured Annie. "As soon as she eats something she'll be fine."

They both watched Natalie bring the plate to a woman Blair didn't recognize. "Who's that?" Blair asked.

Annie was watching, too. "Maggie. She works for Nat."

"That explains the judge's robes. What happened to Peg?"

"Peg's still there," Annie said. "Maggie's a law student. She's just part-time."

"She barely looks old enough to drink."

"She's twenty-four," Annie said.

Maggie was awfully cute. Sandy brown hair, cut very short all around except for the top where it stood up in bleached soft spikes. A square face, big bright laughing eyes. Blair made a note to ask Nat about her later, find out if she was dating anyone.

Annie went off to greet two new arrivals. Blair, on her way to join Tess and Big Bird, saw that they had finally found a comfortable perch near the fireplace, Big Bird semi-reclining on the rolled up living room rug, rather precariously balanced, and Tess near her, leaning back against the wall. They seemed to be having quite a serious discussion, totally oblivious to their attire. Tess absentmindedly fiddled with her tail, or stroked Big Bird's wing with it.

Leah stopped on her way to get some food, and offered to fill a plate for Blair, who declined.

"Are you here alone?" Blair asked. When Leah answered yes, Blair braced herself for the explanation she knew would follow.

"Hildy and I were supposed to come together, but we had one of our fights. I've really been trying to keep my distance, I get so attached, you know, and

17

I've been trying to play it a little looser. I'm not very good at it. She keeps wanting to go out with other women."

Blair only half-listened. More interesting to her was a woman dressed as Fred Astaire, in white tie and tails, completing the outfit with an ivory-handled evening cane and black patent leather pumps.

"I didn't really want to go out with her in the first place, but she kept pushing, you know?" Leah could talk about her relationship problems during a major earthquake. "I was never very good at saying no."

Fred Astaire didn't seem to know too many people. She stood alone near the fireplace.

Leah had to shout to be heard over the din of the music. "I never wanted to see other people, and she always did. That's been our problem from the start."

"Do you know her?" Blair interrupted, nodding in Fred Astaire's direction.

Leah looked at the woman. "She was at that political dinner Natalie dragged us all to. I think her name's Jennifer."

"I thought she looked familiar."

"No, her name's Jessica." But Leah was not to be distracted. "So what do you think I should do? Give her an ultimatum?"

"Just relax," Blair said. "Let her go out with whoever, and you do the same. Life's too short to worry all the time. Enjoy yourself." Ready to follow her own advice, Blair patted Leah on the back and set out to reacquaint herself with Fred Astaire.

Natalie, carrying an orange and green frosted cake, intercepted her. "Do you know them?" Natalie nodded towards two women, neither one in costume.

Both appeared to be having a wonderful time, flirting and dancing with several women.

"I've never seen them before," Blair replied.

That started a round of questioning. It turned out that no one knew these women. They had just seen all the cars in the street and wandered in to check out the party. Though the crashers weren't gay, they realized they had stumbled into something wonderful. They were having a great time, and attracting a lot of attention (Leah in particular, ever attracted to the unavailable). "Let them get their education somewhere else," Natalie muttered to Blair as she went to ask them to leave.

Blair heard clicking behind her, and turned to see Fred Astaire approaching. Blair pointed to the tap shoes. "Do those work?"

The woman did a time-step, finishing with a flourish. Blair applauded. She re-introduced herself, but Jessica remembered her. "Have you eaten yet?" Blair asked.

Jessica shook her head.

"Come on. I was just on my way to get something. Natalie's a fantastic cook."

By midnight the party was going full tilt. Just about everyone was dancing, the volume of the music had increased, the whole house vibrated. Blair took pleasure in watching Jessica: she moved well and didn't take herself too seriously, dancing with abandon. Jessica had applied some sort of glittery powder to her face, and it caught the light and sparkled when she tossed her head.

Tess danced nearby, managing to stay in character, stretching and arching her back with what she must have assumed was feline grace. Her tail kept hitting the woman behind her. Tess was an expansive, good-natured drunk, and she already looked like the cat who had swallowed the canary. She pointed to Big Bird, then shouted over the music to Blair, "Her name's Sarah. Isn't she wonderful! We're going out for dinner next Wednesday."

Blair and Jessica finally had to stop to cool down, and Blair wandered off to get something for them to drink.

"The ice bucket's empty," Annie said. "I'll take it," Blair said, and headed for the freezer which was in the service porch off the main kitchen. She didn't see Natalie and Maggie until she was only a few feet from them.

Natalie had Maggie pressed against the back door, her face buried in Maggie's neck. Maggie's head was tilted back, her eyes closed. Natalie worked her way back to Maggie's mouth. Maggie's judicial robes were open. So was the shirt underneath.

Blair didn't stand there long enough to really see all this. Her eyes made the impression that her mind filled in after she turned around. A sketchy black and white outline that bled into vivid color in a split second. She was also aware of their bodies from the waist down grinding together. She heard the metallic clicks of the mini-blinds as Maggie's hips pressed into them.

Blair retreated a few steps. She had no intention of being the one to break this up.

On her way back to the party, she ran into Annie,

who was headed for the kitchen. "Dance with me," Blair said.

"I'm on a beer run," Annie said, trying to move past her.

But Blair grabbed her arm and pulled her close. "Dance with me first."

They moved slowly together against the rhythm of the record. She could feel Annie's vertebrae through the thin white T-shirt. Annie, bony and fragile.

When Natalie and Maggie rejoined the party, their faces were flushed, their eyes bright. Natalie started to dance, indiscriminately joining couples, shimmying with one, twisting with another, clapping her hands, singing along. She even danced with Maggie.

Blair didn't know if it was a result of what she'd seen, but the mood of the party had changed. A wild, boisterous energy spread through the group. Everyone was dancing by this time, the room pumping to one beat. Blair and Jessica attempted to join the mob, but their energy was on a different level. Blair's ears rang as she and Jessica walked down the driveway to their cars.

Blair waited in Jessica's bed. Jessica was having trouble removing that glittery powder. Lying there, Blair thought about Natalie and Maggie. Her first reaction on discovering them — after the shock wore off — had been cynicism. After ten years, who could blame either Natalie or Annie for an indiscretion at a party? But Natalie was the prime spokeswoman for commitment with a capital C. When Blair closed her eyes, she saw Maggie with that ecstasy on her face. So she opened her eyes. Jessica, instead of removing all the glitter, had added more. Her body glinted in the dim light, its curves accented by powdery shimmers.

Soon Blair's body, too, was glistening. She wondered how the hell she was going to get the stuff off. After a few minutes, she couldn't have cared less.

Sometime later Blair opened her eyes. She slept lightly in someone else's bed, always aware that she wasn't home.

She lay for a moment without moving, Jessica asleep on her shoulder, one leg drawn up over Blair's thighs. Blair's arm had fallen asleep. She knew if she moved it she would wake Jessica. How long had she slept? They hadn't gotten to bed before 1:30, and had made love for a long time.

She stroked Jessica's back, incorporating reaching for her watch in one downward motion, bringing it closer in the upward. 3:35. With some difficulty she managed to put the watch on without disturbing Jessica.

She resumed the stroking, letting her hand move further down, towards Jessica's ass. It lingered there, pressed firmly, traveled back up. She let her other hand wander. She moved it up Jessica's arm, over her shoulder, under her long dark hair to her neck. Back down the front now, between Jessica's breasts, lingering a moment before spreading her fingers across Jessica's smooth stomach.

Jessica let out a little moan. She moved her hips in the rhythm dictated by Blair's hand.

Blair kissed the top of Jessica's head, then her forehead, her eyes, her cheeks. Awake now, Jessica moved on top of Blair, eagerly returning her kisses.

Blair pushed up into the body moving on hers. Her hands held Jessica's hips, kneaded her ass. Her legs spread Jessica's open. She slipped one hand down between Jessica's legs, to be inside her and control her movements at the same time. Jessica raised herself to Blair's hand, then pushed down against Blair's thigh between her legs.

Their exertions left them covered with a fine glaze of moisture; Blair's hand was losing its grip on Jessica's ass. Maybe Jessica said something, but Blair couldn't be sure because everything was shut out of her mind except the area where their bodies were connected. She pushed up, grinding into Jessica, who answered by arching her back, enabling her to push harder against Blair. And then Jessica was coming, slamming into her, colliding with a force that shook cries from Jessica and left both of them breathless afterwards. Jessica remained on top of Blair, her body still moving, though more slowly now, a steady undulating tempo. "What about you?" she whispered into Blair's ear.

"I'm fine. Sleep."

Blair waited until Jessica was breathing evenly before she extricated herself. To murmured protests asking her to stay, Blair got up and dressed quietly. Jessica was asleep before Blair left the room.

• • • • •

Still warm from Jessica's bed, she could see her breath in the air as she walked to her car. Jessica lived on a quiet street of one- and two-story apartment complexes in Studio City. In the four-in-the-morning stillness Blair could sense all those lives shut down for the night. She loved being the only one up and moving. Even the constant breathing of the nearby freeway was almost silent.

By the time she reached the car she was starting to feel the cold. She only put the top up when it rained, or if a passenger insisted. She took a clean towel from the trunk and wiped dew from the front seat, then the windshield. With the windows rolled up, the top down and the heat blasting, she drove home in the cold still night. Warm and tired, she was happiest at times like this, returning home after having left someone's bed.

The streets were empty. Sprinklers were running on some of the center medians; their spray blurred her windshield. The wind blew away the closeness she had experienced with Jessica, cleansed her for her own bed, where she could be safe and alone.

Blair could hear a TV from the unit next to hers. Ted, her neighbor for three years, had AIDS. Lately, no matter what time of night or morning she came home, he was still up. These must be his worst hours. The very reasons that made them so wonderful to Blair — that sense of being the only person alive, of not belonging to anyone — were probably the same ones that made this time so hard on Ted.

Blair went into her dark apartment. Her lights were on timers that had shut off hours earlier. She didn't bother turning any on. She walked straight up to her bedroom. She fell asleep almost immediately.

Chapter Two
Clean-Up

The last guests left after two. A few had offered to help clean up, but Natalie Bazarian was happiest handling her own dirty work, so hadn't let them do much more than dump all the paper plates and plastic cups into big black trash bags. There was still food to put away, some platters to be washed. Natalie liked knowing her task and being able to accomplish it, liked restoring order to the chaos of serving dishes caked with dried sauces, utensils taken out in haste then left where they'd been used. She stood in the kitchen, planning her method of attack.

Annie came up behind her. Wrapped her arms around her saying, "It was a good party."

"Uh-huh."

"I think everyone had fun, don't you?" Annie nuzzled Natalie's neck, ran her hands down her sides.

"Yes." Natalie remained passive, not responding.

"We always give good parties."

Natalie agreed, "We do." But thought: I can't handle this now.

"Can I persuade you to leave the rest till morning?" More kisses, hands coming under Natalie's shirt.

Natalie shrugged herself away. "This won't take long. You go to bed."

Annie didn't protest. "I'm pooped." She kissed Natalie's cheek.

"Turn on the alarm, okay?" Natalie called after her.

Annie mumbled something that sounded like assent as she stumbled off to their bedroom.

Lack of an alarm system had once precipitated a major incident in their relationship. Before they lived together, they alternated nights at each other's apartment. They were at the stage where they spent hours making love, getting up in the morning bleary-eyed and barely able to concentrate on their jobs. Once at Annie's, just lying in bed at two o'clock in the morning, they heard someone trying to get in the side window. Natalie scrambled to call the police, but, "Shh," Annie hissed. Before Natalie could stop her, Annie had bounded out of bed — stark naked, her pale skin luminous in the moonlight — and

27

stomped fearlessly down the hall, banging against the walls, making enough noise to wake the dead, all the while fiercely proclaiming, "You'd better beat it, I'm getting my gun!"

Natalie heard footsteps running from the building.

By the time Annie came back to the bedroom, Natalie had turned on the lamp and was sitting up in bed. The emergency passed, her fear had been replaced by anger. "You could have been killed!"

"Don't be silly," Annie said nonchalantly as she climbed back into bed and inched closer to Natalie.

"Silly? You go charging stark naked into a dark room after a burglar and you're calling *me* silly?"

"What am I supposed to do, let him come in and rob me?"

"How about calling the police?"

"How about 'Good job, Annie, you sure took care of that situation'"

"How about you get an alarm system?"

"What a waste of money!"

"No more of a waste than your gun." Natalie was a staunch supporter of gun control.

"I don't own a gun," Annie said, as if this should have been obvious to Natalie.

"But you were carrying on . . ."

"What was I supposed to say, I'm coming to beat you up?"

Natalie didn't know which infuriated her more, Annie going after an intruder with or without a gun. "I don't want you pulling any stunts like that when we live together," she declared.

That stopped both of them cold. The words were out of her mouth before they had even registered in her head.

"What did you say?"

"You heard me," said Natalie.

They kissed, then moved into each other with such intensity it left them breathless. They took each other to a dark place that was theirs alone. As she gave herself to Annie without reserve, Natalie knew that she was being given the same gift in return. To Natalie this was as concrete a fact as the bed they were lying on: each knew, without speaking, that this, more than any kind of ceremony, was their marriage, their union of body, mind, and spirit. They surfaced from its depths exhausted and content, and slept in each other's arms until morning.

Annie's rashness had been tempered by her years with Natalie. Still, Natalie was glad the house already had an alarm when they moved in.

Annie let Tony, their golden retriever, back inside, and he tore around the living room, madly sniffing the strange smells on the furniture. Natalie filled his water dish, and he lapped noisily as she tackled her mess.

Only when she was alone was it safe to think about what had happened earlier that evening. When she'd looked at Maggie whose head was tilted slightly to one side, a silent question: What? Then the kiss. Finding her way inside Maggie's robe. Her fingers fumbling with the shirt buttons. Then her hands on Maggie's skin. So soft. Bending to kiss Maggie's breast, being held there. Impatiently, eagerly, kissing her way back up to Maggie's neck. Her hands in Maggie's hair — how long she'd wanted to do that! — pulling Maggie's head back more roughly than she'd intended in her haste to find her mouth again.

It was the first time in months she'd felt alive.

At work — and for how long had this been going on? — she was just going through the motions. Slogging through the enormous job of obtaining permits for the three-hundred acre parcel that would become Bridge Creek, a planned community. Six hundred houses of different kinds — condos, apartments, single family residences — plus stores and a small park. There were constant problems and meetings and crises involving streets, sewers, utilities, or land that needed either grading, filling, or cutting. There were environmental groups to deal with, already existing neighborhood organizations to pacify. Plus city councils and boards of supervisors, the chamber of commerce. If no-growth legislation came into effect before they had their final map, the deal was shot. She walked a fine line between magnificent success and total failure.

When Natalie first made the transition into real estate law, she'd thrived on the pressure, she was charged every morning she went to the office. Everything was new, every battle over zoning variances or utility rights or property lines a challenge. Now, playing for higher stakes, she was tired all the time.

And numb from the constant stress. The endless phone calls that came for her at work, in her car, at home. Between Bridge Creek and her other projects, she and Peg, her paralegal, had more than they could handle at the office. And work didn't end there. Natalie attended meetings directly and indirectly relating to the development. If she had lunch with this city councilman or that member of the planning board, would he be able to help with a future problem, expedite a permit or grant a variance?

Natalie took calls at home during the week and on weekends. She was always working.

She'd been telling Annie — and herself — that this wasn't going to go on forever. Just a few more deals, a few more years, and she'd slow down. She drew them forward with a promise of easier times to come. Less stress, less hours at the office. For Annie's birthday one year — two years ago? three? four? — Natalie had bought her a stack of guide books for European cities and countries. They'd pored over the long thin pages for hours, marking and underlining, designing itineraries for different times of the year. If Natalie could get away in the spring, they'd start in Paris, if summer, perhaps the Scandinavian countries. But Natalie hadn't been able to get away at all. Not that spring or summer, and never during the winter. The books had sat out for months, until Annie finally realized that, once again, they weren't going anywhere.

Is this where I thought I'd be at forty? Natalie wondered.

Until now, she'd laughed and told everyone who asked that she associated forty with death. She thought she'd been joking. But as that milestone birthday approached, she found herself subject to wild mood swings, bursts of irrational misdirected anger. She fumed at a man in the express line at the market who had one more than the allowed ten items. When a Volvo suddenly swerved into her lane on the Hollywood Freeway, Natalie had blared her horn, screamed at the driver, then pulled out and passed her. And the poor silver-haired woman, who had probably not seen Natalie, looked genuinely apologetic and mouthed "I'm sorry." Then Natalie

31

had burst into tears because she'd hurt some stranger's feelings.

Whenever she told Annie "next spring" or "as soon as this project is finished" she heard echoes of her father making similar promises to her mother. Her father had never slowed down. After his heart attack he made an attempt at keeping shorter hours at the office, going in late, coming home early, but soon had stretched back to his normal ten-hour day. Years ago her mother had learned to plan vacations that would keep him away from phones and office contact — photo safaris in Africa, following the ancient silk route in China, trips down the Nile.

Annie didn't go so far as making travel plans, and she never complained. Not when Natalie had to cancel their plans because of meetings with clients, not when Natalie worked through a weekend. Annie merely booked herself for more editing time; she could be busy round the clock if she chose to. And sometimes, depending on Natalie's schedule, she chose to.

But Annie owned the editing house. Natalie didn't have the luxury of creating her own timetable. Her projects bled into each other, cases overlapped. And her best intentions didn't hold up against the pressures from the firm, from her own inner self that wouldn't let her pass up an interesting or challenging case.

Natalie hadn't taken a real vacation — the week in Chicago when her father had his heart attack didn't count — in years. A weekend here and there, often scheduled around a visit to a site. But no extended time to be with Annie.

Did that explain why she'd stood in her own

32

kitchen earlier that evening and pawed at someone practically young enough to be her daughter?

About a month earlier, after a particularly grueling weekend spent working, Peg had called the law school placement office for some temporary paralegal help, just to work on the Bridge Creek project. At first, Natalie thought Maggie the answer to all her prayers.

Maybe a sixth sense about the third year law student told her Maggie was gay. Maggie sported a suitably tailored outfit for the interview, and had arranged her extremely short hair into an acceptably punky style. She wore one pair of earrings in one ear, and a completely different, and lone, earring in the other. Barely passable for the conservative standards of Morris, Madison & Stein.

But Maggie was bright and diligent. And, equally important, thorough, a must for the kind of detailed work she had to do. Plus, she worked extra hours. Neither Morris, Madison, nor Stein could argue with that.

Natalie's suspicions about her clerk's lifestyle were confirmed one evening when they were working late, reviewing the Declaration of Covenants, Conditions, and Restrictions for Bridge Creek. It was a massive job, and Maggie was making note of the changes when the phone rang. Natalie answered it. A woman's voice asked to speak to Maggie. Absorbed in the CC&R's in front of her, Natalie handed the receiver to Maggie. "I'll be over later . . . When we're *done*, Sydney . . . I can't talk now." When Maggie hung up, her face was flushed. She turned to Natalie. "Sorry. I told her she wasn't supposed to call me here."

"No problem." Natalie smiled.

"That's what you think," Maggie commented dryly.

Natalie sensed an opening into a more personal realm. "These things always blow over," she commented noncommittally.

"Not this time. Sometimes a person can love you too much." Maggie looked straight at Natalie and said, "You know how some women can be."

No need to guess anymore. Natalie was surprised at the thrill she felt.

"I hope you don't mind my asking . . ." Maggie's voice trailed off.

"What?"

"The picture on your desk."

After years of living and working in the straight world, Natalie had learned when she could trust someone. "That's Annie, my lover."

"That's what I thought, but I wasn't sure if I should say anything. Not everyone wants their cover blown."

"I don't need a cover."

"Okay," Maggie backed down. "I guess I wanted to know why you stay here. I know you're a partner and all, but doesn't this place get to you?"

"What do you mean?"

"The atmosphere. It's so straight."

"I just want to do my work."

"Yeah, but this firm has a pretty stuffy reputation. When they told me about the job, I almost didn't come for the interview."

"I'm glad you did."

"Me too." Maggie smiled. "But I was really surprised to find you here."

Now Natalie was surprised. Maggie continued. "I didn't think I'd find a dyke who was a partner."

"Did I give you the secret handshake or something?" Natalie asked.

"Wouldn't it be great if there was one. No, I'm just good at picking up signals. Besides —" Again Maggie smiled. "You knew about me the first time we met."

"I did?"

"Sure. Why else would you hire me?"

"Your record and your resumé —"

Maggie cut her off. "There must be a thousand equally qualified law students you could have picked, over half of whom would look more appropriate."

Natalie had to agree with her.

"No," Maggie continued, "you just wanted to work with a dyke."

"That wasn't how I thought about it."

Maggie studied her a moment. "I'm sure it wasn't," she said with a sly smile.

Work went on as usual after that night. Natalie felt very good about their progress. She had to acknowledge that the good feelings were due in part to working with another gay person. It wasn't the kind of thing she usually thought much about, but appreciated when it was there. And it made a difference. There was an unspoken bond between her and Maggie.

The day Natalie found out that they'd gotten their tentative map approved, one of the minor victories in the long process of permitting a development, she felt like celebrating. Annie had a late edit, so Natalie left Maggie a message inviting her to dinner that night. After all, her law clerk's involvement had been crucial to their success.

Maggie met her at the office at six-thirty. "Am I too early? You look surprised to see me."

"You're right on time." Natalie fumbled with the papers on her desk so she wouldn't have to look up again until she was absolutely ready. When Maggie came in to work she wore her office uniform, tailored outfits in keeping with the unspoken dress code of Morris, Madison & Stein. Now, clearly, she had chosen from her real wardrobe. A loose blouse hung attractively over grey pants. A butter-soft black leather jacket was stylishly cut with padded shoulders and full sleeves. Normally law students couldn't afford clothes like that — were these presents from too-loving Sydney? Maggie's earrings were huge hammered silver disks. She was a knockout.

Almost as soon as they sat down to dinner at an Italian restaurant near the office Maggie started talking about her lover, as if she'd been waiting for this opportunity since the first night she and Natalie had worked late.

"Is Sydney an attorney too?" Natalie asked.

"No, Sydney's independently wealthy."

"So she doesn't work."

"Well, let's just say she dabbles. When I first met her, she made jewelry. She made these earrings."

Natalie studied the huge silver disks. "They're beautiful." They were all the jewelry Maggie needed. They accentuated her face, her huge cat eyes.

"They are. But now she's designing furniture." Maggie thought for a second. "Or is it lamps?"

"You don't know?"

"It's hard to keep up — it changes from month to month."

"How long have you been together?"

"We met right before I started law school. I moved in a few months later. She's got an incredible house in Malibu."

"That must be nice."

"It was. I moved out a few months ago. Sydney never liked the idea of sharing me with law school. She feels she's entitled to more of my time. And my love."

"So you're breaking up?"

"Let's just say we're re-structuring our relationship." Maggie sipped her wine. "How about you?"

Natalie told Maggie how long she and Annie had been together.

"That must be some kind of record."

"There are more of us out there than you think," Natalie countered. She didn't add that sometimes the responsibility of being a model to many of their friends was more than she could handle.

"Did you know right away that this was it?"

"Annie says she knew, but it took me a little longer." Not until that moment Annie went charging down the hall after the burglar had Natalie realized the depth of her feelings. "But it was so long ago, who can remember?"

Reluctant to talk about Annie with Maggie, Natalie steered the conversation in a different direction, never too hard to do with law students. They always loved to talk about the law.

"Nothing personal," Maggie said, "but real estate law isn't for me. Aside from all the details — CC&R's, forget it — I don't think I could be so closeted. Doesn't it make you claustrophobic?"

Natalie thought they'd already had this conversation; still, she couldn't help but feel defensive. "You've seen how I'm treated, not any differently than anyone else around here."

"But don't you feel different from everyone else?"

"Because I'm gay? I'd say what everyone around here has in common is the law, not their sexual orientation. I probably share more with the straightest, most conservative lawyer in this firm than I do with half the gay women I'd meet in a bar."

"Sure, in that you'd probably have more to talk about with a bunch of lawyers. But don't you think you'd share more history with the dykes in the bar? Be honest."

"What does that have to do with anything? I like my work." At least she had when she first started, but Natalie never conceded anything in a debate. "I make a very good living, I've got a supportive lover and friends." For whose benefit was this little recitation, she wondered. "The minor sacrifices, no, compromises, are worth it." Five years ago she could have given a speech that would have Maggie up and applauding. Now she could barely convince herself of the merits of her life.

"I don't know," Maggie said. "There are just too many specific gay issues that need to be addressed. I think I'd feel like an impostor doing anything else." Maggie talked about her plans to become involved in

38

various gay organizations after law school. She was going to make her living helping her community.

Despite her own slightly defensive stance, Natalie found Maggie's enthusiasm infectious, it made her remember the excitement of her early days as an attorney. They had so much to talk about and were in such good spirits they spent almost two hours over dinner.

Natalie tried to interest Maggie in splitting a dessert, but Maggie said she was full. "That sauce on the fish was really rich. Delicious, though."

"I think he puts a touch of fennel in it," Natalie said.

"I wouldn't have guessed."

"The trick is to put in enough to add a little flavor, but not so much as to make it recognizable. That's what adds the mystery."

"You should have been a chef," Maggie said jokingly.

"That's actually what I wanted to do for a while. No one took me seriously though, everyone assumed I was going to be a lawyer like my father. I guess I did, too." Natalie had never told anyone about her secret dreams of becoming a chef. Once she'd mentioned it to her mother, who had laughed and said, "You're too smart to spend all your time cooking. And believe me, you'll do enough of it for your husband and children." Natalie hadn't had the nerve to tell her mother she was serious, that it wasn't so much about cooking as it was about creating an environment in which people could enjoy themselves.

"The closest I came to my dream was investing in a restaurant some friends opened. Oh well." Natalie sighed and took a last sip of her espresso. She realized she'd been excited throughout the meal, eager and animated the way she'd be with a new friend. Or lover.

After dinner, Natalie drove Maggie back to her car. Before she got out, Maggie said thank you and leaned over to kiss Natalie on the cheek. Natalie had just turned to Maggie to say good night, so their lips met. Just lightly. Innocently. But then they lingered a few seconds, past innocence. "Congratulations again," Maggie said. "Good night." Then the slam of the car door.

Natalie waited until Maggie's car started before she pulled out into the street. She was stunned and embarrassed by her reaction to the kiss. She reached her hand to her lips. Thought of Maggie's lips: soft, slightly open. She couldn't read the kiss; she'd had wine, Maggie had had wine. Probably nothing to it. A kiss like that after an evening like theirs probably signified as much as a warm handshake after you haven't seen someone in a long time. She reminded herself that she was almost forty years old. That Maggie was only twenty-four. Still, Natalie felt stirrings of an excitement she hadn't experienced since she first met Annie.

Since that night, Natalie had kept what she called her little infatuation to herself. That brief moment was all she had really needed to maintain an innocent fantasy that would satisfy her until it faded on its own.

It inspired her to start up her fitness regimen again, rising early to work out with an exercise video tape, or to take a brisk walk up the hill. Annie had never needed to exercise. Usually when Natalie got on one of her kicks Annie would go along to keep her company, and Annie would lose weight, and Annie would stick with the exercise long after Natalie had grown bored with it and stopped. Now Natalie had a new impetus to firm up. She used to have a good body. At her age, it was a little harder to whip it into shape. Harder, but not impossible.

When she was away from the office, she reasoned with herself constantly, making the case for her immunity to Maggie. When she realized she was talking about Maggie to Annie, she stopped herself. She'd meticulously constructed her life around work and Annie. She'd had crushes before. They were never serious. She'd always viewed them as minor nuisances on the way to her life's goal — retirement with Annie — and so could always talk herself out of them. But abstract logic and lectures couldn't compete with concrete physical reactions. She looked forward to the days Maggie was going to be coming in. She memorized whatever outfit Maggie wore. Often she would be so busy they wouldn't see much of each other, but just the sight of Maggie's backpack stuffed in a corner of the office cheered her.

Annie had been the one to suggest inviting Maggie to the Halloween party. "There'll be a lot of single women you can introduce her to." As if to prove to herself that this was just a silly infatuation, Natalie had encouraged Maggie to come. "And bring Sydney." But Maggie had shown up alone.

And then those crazy moments in the kitchen. Was that what she'd wanted since that quick kiss in the car?

She had finished the dishes. She dried and put away the platters, the big coffee urn. She surveyed her kitchen. There was nothing more she could do tonight.

In the ten years she'd been with Annie she'd never come so close to ruining everything. She was just lucky that no one had walked in on her and Maggie. That one out of control minute could have cost her her carefully constructed life.

Natalie resolved that this wouldn't go any further. She'd have Sunday and Monday to collect herself, then on Tuesday she'd tell Maggie that she'd just gotten carried away. Apologize. Things would be awkward for a while, but that would pass. She'd get back on track. Take Annie somewhere romantic for a long weekend, maybe back to San Francisco, or to the wine country. Or maybe save the time and go somewhere really spectacular for a week or ten days. That was it, ten days for their tenth anniversary.

Natalie turned off the lights as she walked back to the bedroom. Annie was sound asleep. Natalie lay back on her pillow, arms under her head. She remembered how Maggie had moved under her hands. Imagined what it would be like to feel Maggie stretched out on top of her. Tried unsuccessfully to replace Maggie with Annie. Her guilt kept her on her side of the bed.

The hour glowed blue from the clock radio. Almost three-thirty and still she wasn't tired. In time, she knew, she could kill these feelings. Everything was at stake. She would make herself numb until she no longer responded to Maggie. She swore from this moment that's what she'd do.

She slept fitfully. She finally gave up around seven o'clock and got out of bed. She picked up the paper, but wasn't in much shape to read it. She made a pot of coffee and took her cup into the living room.

The house looked different even though she'd put everything back in place. Almost too neat. The only visible trace of the party was the rug rolled against the wall. Other hints lingered in the air, echoes of last night's mixture of noise and perfume. The sun brightened but didn't warm the patio yet. She let Tony out. He tore up the hill after a bird or squirrel that she couldn't see. She closed the doors before lying down on the couch.

She must have dozed, because it was nine-thirty when she heard Annie moving around the kitchen. She stumbled in to say good morning.

"Hi, sleepy. I made a fresh pot of coffee." Annie poured her a cup, handed it to her with a kiss. "What time did you finally come to bed?"

"Around three, I think."

"I felt you tossing and turning. Did you get any sleep?"

"Not much."

They sat around drinking coffee and reading the paper. Rather, Annie read and Natalie pretended to concentrate until, too restless to sit still, she offered to make breakfast. "How about pecan waffles?"

"You did all that cooking for the party. How about plain old toast and jam?"

But Natalie won out. She always did when it came to food.

Annie wanted to go to an afternoon movie. Natalie knew that in the dark she'd be prey to thoughts of Maggie. Maybe if she got away by herself for a few hours first. "I have to spend a little time at the office."

"You said you wouldn't have to go in this weekend."

Did Annie suspect anything? "I'm going to be out at the site all day tomorrow and I forgot to leave my notes for Peg. If I go now, it'll save me from having to go in at the crack of dawn." Seeing Annie's disappointed look, she relented. "What if I meet you at the theater?"

Annie reluctantly agreed. Natalie went to shower. She didn't really want to go to the office, but she couldn't think of another legitimate way to find the privacy she so desperately needed. Only out of Annie's sight did she feel safe. She was sure that Annie could read her thoughts, could sense that something was wrong. It didn't matter that Annie hadn't said anything. Natalie couldn't count the times she'd been about to speak when Annie would suddenly say the exact thing that Natalie had been thinking. Maybe she should tell Annie what had happened. Tell her it was because of a couple of hits of grass and the drinks and make less of it, laugh it off as the first sign of a mid-life crisis. She could tell Annie that it had happened and that it had scared her, because it wasn't what she wanted, Annie and their life together was what she wanted. But then what? What if Annie didn't understand, or got jealous? This wasn't important, Natalie kept telling herself. She would just stick to her numbing routine until she got back on track.

She bargained, as she had the night before: let me keep a flicker of this fantasy, that's all, just until I'm settled back into my life. Then, as soon as construction on Bridge Creek has started, she and Annie would go on a second honeymoon and life would be wonderful again.

But not even a hot shower followed by an ice cold rinse could wash away her apprehension that whatever had gotten hold of her wasn't that easily banished.

Morris, Madison & Stein took up half of the fifteenth floor of an office building in Santa Monica. The suite had that extra quiet of Sunday about it, the reception area tidy, all the magazines neatly arrayed. Natalie walked down the hall, past the copy room and the library. She sat at her desk and looked out the window. She could see no signs of life on the deserted side street. No pedestrians, not even a jogger. No cars drove by. A helicopter thudded overhead; Natalie scanned the sky but never caught a glimpse of it.

Though airy and spacious, her office seemed dim and cramped when she turned back to it. Her heavy reference books crowded the shelves. Files stacked on her desk left her little room to work. Cardboard storage boxes overflowing with still more files lined the walls, reminders of how much backlog there was. So her being here today had at least some basis in fact.

She couldn't remember when there hadn't been a bigger stack of "To Do" than "To File." She had been practicing law for fifteen years, twelve of them with this firm. She had no idea anymore whether or not she liked it. It was no longer a question of that. She had certain commitments and responsibilities. She'd become the opposite of Maggie who needed only her love of the law for motivation and inspiration.

Natalie sat. She paced. She needed to diffuse her energy, but she couldn't think of anywhere else to go. She picked up the phone and dialed Blair's number. The machine came on and she hung up. She needed to talk to someone. But who? She realized that she rarely called her friends just to talk. Annie took care of their social calendar, and filled her in on what everyone was up to. And lately Annie had had to check with Natalie's secretary, Sandra, to find out whether or not Natalie was free to have dinner with their friends. Natalie used to have lunch with Blair once or twice a month, but she'd had to cancel their last few dates because of work. She had no life outside the office. It wasn't just Annie — she'd lost touch with everyone.

Her eyes wandered to the framed photograph of Annie and herself that she kept on her desk. Taken six or seven summers earlier, it was of the two of them on a hike in the Santa Monica mountains. She'd propped the camera on a rock, set the automatic timer, and rushed back to Annie. They were both laughing when the shutter clicked.

She still had vivid memories of that day. They'd packed a lunch, found a perfect spot for their picnic, and spent several hours there, eating, dozing, making love.

Natalie studied the picture closely. They'd been exercising a lot that summer, running, biking, playing tennis. They'd been in great shape, tanned and healthy. Their house had been filled with friends, gatherings that had started informally, one or two people dropping in on their way home from the beach, or after running errands. Afternoons became evenings as they sat outside until it was too dark to see, their white shirts glowing in the shadowless light. They'd talked into the night until Natalie went into the kitchen to make pasta with lots of fresh vegetables for all of them. The smell of fresh basil always reminded her of that summer, bringing with it the memory of a hint of warmth in the air.

That seemed like another lifetime.

She heard a noise in the reception area. Her adrenaline surged. The photograph was in a heavy silver frame; if worse came to worst she could use it as a weapon. She crept to the door. Flattening herself against the wall, she took a deep breath and raised the frame above her head, ready to bring it down on whoever was planning to separate her from her office equipment.

Maggie peeked in the doorway.

Both women jumped.

"Christ, Maggie, you scared me! I thought you were a burglar."

"Are you all right?"

"I will be, once my tachycardia subsides." Natalie was leaning back against the wall, arms at her side,

47

the photograph still in her hand. She took a moment to catch her breath. "What are you doing here?"

"I remembered you hadn't left any notes for Peg on the easements." They faced each other awkwardly. "Maybe I'd better leave."

But before she could turn, Natalie grabbed her arm, held it fast. "Not yet."

Had she somehow willed this to happen? Did she even believe that was possible? Maggie's wrist in her hand was cool and smooth. No one, ever, with such soft skin. Natalie's thumb moved up and down the inside of the wrist. If something's going to happen, it's going to happen for a long time. If nothing's going to happen, what's one more kiss? She wanted that more than anything. "About last night . . ." Abruptly she dropped Maggie's arm and moved towards the window. She couldn't be so close to her and think at the same time. She realized she was still holding the photograph of her and Annie. Without looking at it, she put it back on the desk.

Maggie broke the long silence. "I was thinking . . ."

Natalie turned to listen.

"We both know real estate isn't my thing. I should be working in family law, or discrimination, something more grass roots oriented." Maggie moved closer to Natalie, not touching her, but so close that Natalie could feel the charge between them. "So much needs to be done," Maggie continued, tiger eyes wide and bright. "Civil rights, gay partnerships and families, civil disobedience, sodomy law reform, sexual orientation legislation. The field's wide open." Maggie paused.

The kid was good, Natalie found herself thinking.

48

Already she used her hands like a politician making a campaign speech. And what she said was true. Natalie's friend Delia Owens was practicing just this kind of law, was regularly quoted in the news, and was winning landmark decisions for her clients. Natalie was thinking how well Maggie would do with Delia and so she was totally unprepared for Maggie's punch line.

"We could do it together," Maggie whispered, and the excitement in her voice was a combination of idealism and sexuality.

Natalie couldn't believe what she was hearing.

"You've got the experience, the political connections. I know the grass roots side. Do you want to subdivide parcels of land so that more people can live in houses that look exactly the same and shop in chain stores that have no character? Step in one of those places — it could be anywhere. Is that the contribution you want to make? Is that the kind of environment you dreamed of creating? We could make changes that would affect people's lives for the better."

For one impetuous moment Natalie allowed herself the fantasy. She couldn't live in it for very long, however. Maggie's life was simple and uncomplicated, uncluttered by the career and personal commitments in which Natalie was mired. She knew Maggie wouldn't understand about compromise. Just as she knew that for herself a change of that magnitude was unthinkable.

Natalie envied Maggie her black and white view of the world. Everything seemed so easy for her. And she had no doubt Maggie would achieve her goals. In a few years, Natalie knew, Maggie would be one of the four or five activist attorneys always quoted in the paper or interviewed on the news any time there was an event that touched the gay community.

With a shocking immediacy, Natalie's need came to her, fully formed and palpable. She couldn't change her life, but she could, for a few moments, possess this woman and her vital energy and passion. While one part of her was giving herself a lecture on commitment, another part was moving towards Maggie, fully resolved. Her movements came from a place without words. Commitment was just a word, an abstraction. Reality was Maggie, here in the doorway, standing as she'd stood in the kitchen last night, that same question in her eyes. But instead Natalie heard herself saying "I know just the firm for you. I'll write you a recommendation."

If possible, the office was even quieter after Maggie left. The stillness became a pressure around Natalie that deadened all sound. She could feel her heart pounding in her head.

She straightened the folders on her desk. Not that anything was out of place, she just felt a need to be busy, have her hands touching things.

What had stopped her from doing what she'd so desperately wanted? What kept her entrenched in her life?

Conversely, what did she have to complain about? She was living the American dream — or at least a variation of it.

This was not the first time she'd questioned her choices, wavered in her course. But she couldn't understand why she was unable to pull or force herself through it this go-round. She'd always been able to hang on, white-knuckling it through whatever rough situation she faced. Waiting for her, she knew, was the comforting realization that she was in fact happy with her life. But that other shore, formerly so easily attainable, had become another country. Annie was in that other country. Natalie had somehow wandered off along the border, walking in the same direction as Annie, but suddenly there was this river between them. What was going on?

She called Annie. "Hon, do you mind?"

"I knew this would happen." Annie sounded more disappointed than angry. This wasn't the first movie Natalie had missed because of work.

"There's more here than I thought," Natalie said. "Why don't you go without me." She promised to be home by six and hung up. She'd never lied to Annie before. She'd hardly recognized her own voice.

Chapter Three
The First Shoe

About the time Annie and Natalie first moved in together, one of the attorneys Natalie worked with developed a crush on her. Natalie, when she finally told Annie about it, admitted to having been afraid of Annie's reaction. But Annie was so secure in their relationship that she wasn't at all jealous. She was even a little flattered that someone else was infatuated with her Natalie. Over the years, each had confessed little crushes, flutters they called them, on women they knew. All meaningless, having no bearing on their lives or relationship. Now Annie waited for the moment Natalie would laugh and tell her, Guess who has a crush on me now?

How else could she explain Natalie's behavior? Her distraction, the annoyance with which she greeted even the slightest favor Annie asked. Annie was already accustomed to Natalie's lack of demonstrative affection when they were in public. It had taken some getting used to when they were first together, but now she accepted it as a fact of life, and not as a barometer of Natalie's feelings for her. In this period of distance, however, Annie felt the lack more acutely, harking back to their early days together, before she understood that that's just how Natalie was.

She tried to imagine Natalie coming to her and saying there was someone else. What would I do, Annie thought. Give her an ultimatum — her or me? After ten years, things weren't so simple.

From the first night they met Annie Weiss knew that this was the person she was going to grow old with. She knew without knowing how she knew.

Annie had dated lots of women, few of whom were Jewish, and had never noticed anything missing until she started going out with Natalie. Not that Natalie was Jewish, but she made Annie realize that what these other women had lacked was a background similar to hers. Religion wasn't the key ingredient here; family and tradition were among the factors that drew her to Natalie, were what they had in common. Annie had been shaped more by the cultural than the religious aspects of being Jewish. From her family she had learned loyalty and support, knew that even if you didn't like these people so much, you still loved them, they were home.

Natalie's Armenian family was the same way.

"Call me Rose," Mrs. Bazarian said the first time she met Annie, who, a little nervous, didn't call her anything for the first two days of their long Thanksgiving weekend in Chicago.

Meeting Natalie's parents gave Annie a new perspective on Natalie. Natalie's father obviously respected Natalie's legal expertise, he often asked her opinion on a case, but let her try to put logs on the fire and "No, not like that. Be careful. Here, let me do it."

Natalie's mother was the same way. When it was time to make dinner their first night there, Natalie asked if there was anything she could do to help. "You can make the salad," her mother said.

"Any particular kind?" Natalie asked.

"Anything you want."

Natalie put some water on the stove to boil, and started cutting up broccoli.

"You're going to put that in the salad?" her mother asked skeptically.

"Do you not want me to?"

"Make it any way you want. We just usually have lettuce and tomatoes and cucumber. And your father likes a little scallion, too."

"Is that how you want me to make it?"

"It's your salad."

For the rest of the weekend Annie watched in amusement as Natalie switched back and forth between the powerhouse, career-oriented lawyer Annie was used to and someone's daughter, treated alternately as adult and child.

Natalie's parents lived in the wealthy Chicago suburb of Lake Forest. On Thanksgiving day they drove into the city for dinner at Mrs. Bazarian's sister's. Aunty Iris lived with her husband Hank in an apartment building on Lake Shore Drive.

When the elevator opened onto the hallway of Aunty Iris's floor, Annie understood with a shock the familiarity of the situation. The cooking odors wafting through the corridor reminded her of those she'd encountered on holiday visits with her own family. She couldn't smell them without remembering standing outside the door to one or another aunt's apartment, the faint sound of the doorbell, the responding commotion it set off within, the clamoring to answer the door, cries of Who is it, the background noises of uncles and aunts and cousins, a great racket and din that hit them with full force as the door opened and they were drawn into the apartment redolent of brisket and noodle kugel. The aromas in this hallway brought back Aunt Hannah's whispered hints to "Try the chicken fricassee, I made that. Don't bother with the stuffed cabbage, that's Sophie's."

At Aunty Iris's, a young cousin greeted them at the door, an enthusiastic boy, about eleven, face flushed, shirt untucked, shoes off. "Jimmy, you've gotten so big I hardly recognized you," Natalie exclaimed. Jimmy shyly endured this admiration and an introduction to Annie before blurting out eagerly, "Uncle Robert's teaching me how to do a handstand!" and hurrying back to his lesson.

Once inside the apartment, Annie felt immediately at home. The people she met could have been her own relatives; vibrant older women, in their silk blouses and slacks, their grey or dyed hair fashionably cut, bustling from another room to see who was here at last, fawning over Natalie: "Let me look at you," "You look terrific," "L.A. must agree with you." Welcoming Annie with "Any friend of Natalie's . . ."

Their greetings were almost drowned out by a loud argument taking place in the corner.

"That's like saying the homeless want to be out on the street, Jack," a moustached man was yelling at his adversary.

"I'm not saying that at all," Jack shouted, shaking his head. "But giving them money isn't going to help anything. What did we have when we came to this country, nothing."

"Please, not that same old argument."

Natalie interrupted her uncles to introduce them to Annie. "And in this corner, wearing the red, white, and blue of the Republican party, we have Uncle Jack. And, in the pastels of the wishy-washy liberal Democrats, Uncle Souran."

"Ah, the reinforcements have arrived. Natalie, drum some sense into this man," Souran said.

"Uncle Souran, Uncle Jack and I will never agree on politics." Natalie kissed both men. "I have learned to accept him with all his faults." They all laughed.

"Excuse us, Annie," said florid-faced Souran. "My brother and I always talk like this to each other. We haven't come to blows. Yet."

But Annie was used to this. The men reminded her of her uncles Bill and Milton, whose violent arguments weren't confined to politics; they could not have a civilized conversation if their lives depended on it. Yet, fiercely loyal, each would defend the other against all comers.

56

Annie understood families like Natalie's. Chaos and the volume up high, exhaustion when everyone finally went home. That was a typical family gathering. A table laid with platters for an army she could relate to. Leftovers for days. What she could never understand was dinner with exactly enough food for the number of guests present. People politely waiting their turn to speak.

That first trip reenforced Annie's belief that she and Natalie were meant to be together forever. Over the years, Natalie's family had become as important to Annie as any other aspect of their life together. This bond was one of the foundations on which they had built their relationship.

When they were first together, Annie used to have fantasies of something terrible happening to Natalie. Her embarrassment at these thoughts didn't keep her from having them, she'd been so afraid of losing the perfect happiness they had. When had that happiness changed? Annie had no incident on which to pin the beginning of Natalie's distance.

Until recently, she hadn't imagined they could be separated by anything other than death. They had been through everything already — all the battles and skirmishes, the smoothing out and shaping and sizing of the cloth that was their relationship. That was why they'd had a commitment ceremony on their fifth anniversary, to reaffirm their intentions, to make a public declaration of their private feelings.

Right after that Annie left the company she'd been with for ten years and opened her own editing house. She worked sixty hour weeks, putting all the money she earned back into the state-of-the-art equipment. She went through tremendous bouts of depression — could she keep the business going, was she making the right move? Natalie was occasionally jealous of Annie's time, but mostly was supportive. Annie wasn't a hustler, but she was a good and talented editor, and she built her business through hard, hard work.

Those years had been an adjustment in their lives. Not a growing apart, but a realignment. And although the cloth frayed and stretched, the relationship always held. Annie thought they'd come together stronger and more sure of it than ever.

Experience had taught her that outside problems can weigh so heavily on a relationship that the crisis became everything, capable of consuming everything they gave it, and "I love you" fell into a chasm between them. She knew they'd been through stretches of distance before, periods in which one of them had wandered off — not literally, just been distracted for a time.

But those times had always passed before.

Once Annie's biggest fear of committing herself to one person was the worry that someone else would come along, someone more interesting, or funnier, or sexier to her. Or just someone else. But all that wanderlust had evaporated after she met Natalie. It had been years since she had any interest in sleeping with other women — before Natalie, something she'd done pretty casually. She was no longer willing to share that kind of intimacy. If she found someone attractive, she had no need to act on any impulses. She had thought the same applied for Natalie.

They hadn't made love in weeks. Most of the time Annie woke in the morning after Natalie had already left for the office. She vaguely remembered being kissed and murmured to, a lingering of Natalie's perfume.

Since the party, Natalie's withdrawal was complete. They rattled around the house, spending their time in separate rooms. They weren't living together. They merely inhabited the same space.

Sometimes Annie caught herself living in their past, remembering. As if Natalie were already gone.

Chapter Four
Mirror, Mirror

Am I next? Natalie wondered as she watched Jack Korbin, one of the top tax lawyers in Hollywood (and a senior partner at Madison, Morris & Stein), fidget in his seat at the Tuesday morning partners' meeting. He had just bought a huge estate in the Palisades. He owned a house in Palm Desert and a condo at Vail, but that didn't stop him and his wife from taking at least one European vacation a year. He was living a life others only dreamed about. And his stress-related skin condition was acting up; he itched all over. Natalie watched as Jack Korbin reached into a pocket of his custom-made suit to extract his Alupent inhaler. On top of everything else, at age fifty-eight, he had developed asthma.

Natalie studied the faces gathered around the polished conference table.

Cassandra Ryder yawned. She had recently made partner. But at what cost? She flirted with Epstein-Barr, also called the Yuppie virus, a debilitating relative of mononucleosis.

Hank Stein, son of founding partner Jacob Stein, rolled his head constantly, stretching his neck, popping vertebrae. At the end of a particularly trying day, his right eye would twitch uncontrollably.

Matthew Madison, the other senior partner, while possessing no particular tics or twitches, was the most immobile person Natalie had ever encountered. He always looked as if he were wearing a neck brace. When someone spoke, Matthew Madison would twist his upper body in the direction of the voice, and then his head would follow. Behind his back everyone called him The Statue.

When Natalie looked around the room she saw not some of the top attorneys in their field but twitching, itching, insomniac bundles of nerves. And she included herself in that huddled mass.

She displayed no obvious physical signs. Her only problem so far was a disturbing memory loss. More than a matter of forgetting, a black hole resided in place of her retrieval mechanism. This had been going on for several months, and she was learning to compromise, to substitute a word for the one she'd lost. Her initial panic and disorientation had given way to frustration and annoyance.

The voice of The Statue suddenly boomed in her direction. Known for his courtroom oratory, The Statue always seemed to have the precise word at his disposal. Now he skewed his body to face in Natalie's direction. "And how is your development coming?" he asked.

"Quite well," Natalie bluffed.

"Your master CC&R's are finished?"

"Not yet."

By making no further comment, The Statue created an uncomfortable silence that generated a desire to explain, to offer more information than was necessarily prudent.

"Things got a little hectic after my assistant left. I'm just catching up now."

"How about letting Parker Sherman have a crack at the first draft. He's sharp, that boy."

As much as Natalie hated to admit that she wasn't finished with the first draft yet, it was even harder for her to accept Parker Sherman's help to do it.

He was a second-year associate, a real hot-shot, hired right out of law school on the basis of his outstanding academic record and impressive presence. He was very bright. And sharp. And Natalie disliked him. When someone else's shit hit the fan, Parker always seemed to be around to step in and save the day, sometimes as a result of sheer luck, but more often than not due to his own clever maneuvering. People like Parker Sherman knew when to play to someone's weakness, when to play to a strength.

62

From the start he'd known which partners to cultivate, which to respect from afar. Right away he'd ingratiated himself with co-workers, especially the secretaries and paralegals, so that they were even willing to stay late for him, do extra work.

What Natalie resented most was that advancements she had struggled for were automatically granted to Parker Sherman. Men like Sherman, given no handicap in the world's eyes, started out with big ones in Natalie's.

It galled her to have to ask him for help. Her discomfort made her offer feeble excuses. "I've been behind the eight ball the last few weeks. Swamped here, can't sleep at home."

Parker listened sympathetically. "It's my pleasure, really," he'd said. "And an honor. I was hoping we could work together sometime. You can teach me so much."

Unctuous, but not fawning. All innocence — but Natalie knew he wouldn't hesitate to walk over her to get what he wanted. She would have to watch out for Parker Sherman.

One more worry to keep her up at night. She always had trouble sleeping when she was under a lot of pressure. Before, without Maggie to help her wade through it, Natalie had been buried under massive amounts of paperwork for Bridge Creek. But she knew the root cause of her insomnia was not how much work had piled up. She was upset over Maggie and could no longer control her moods. Look at how sloppy she'd been lately. Never before had she let anything interfere with her performance at work. She'd have an easier time staying on her toes if she could only get some sleep. Maybe having Parker

Sherman breathing down her neck would help her regain her edge.

And with him on board, as much as she hated to admit it, a lot of the mess of Bridge Creek would get straightened out. She had arranged a meeting at the site for the following Monday, making it possible for her and Annie to have a long weekend in Palm Springs. She'd set up lunch with Jeremy Ives, the developer, to brief him on her plans.

Jeremy was a type she would avoid at parties. His expensive clothes were too studiedly hip, and his self-assurance came across as arrogance. But then he had earned the self-assurance, betting years ago on Riverside County as the next burgeoning community within an hour's drive of L.A. Now, with Bridge Creek and similar projects he was reaping the rewards of his prescience.

He had chosen the location for the meeting, a casually elegant and pricey restaurant near the beach. Very trendy L.A.: minimal amount of art on the crisp white walls, no coverings on the hard slate floors. Natalie wished for a more subdued location. She had a headache which was aggravated by the din in this particular spot. Noise bounced off the bright surfaces of everything, was as blinding as the sun pouring through the skylights, flashing off a knife blade, a serving platter.

Jeremy was waiting for her, and the maitre d' led them to a table set for three.

"Who's joining us?" Natalie asked. She was used to Jeremy's bringing people along with him, business associates, contractors, politicians. He liked having a woman attorney, and sometimes liked to show Natalie off.

"I've asked your associate to join us. Didn't he tell you?"

Natalie covered quickly. "I've been in meetings all morning."

"I invited him yesterday," Jeremy said, "when he called me with his questions."

Natalie had no one but herself to blame for this, and kicked herself for being so sloppy. Wednesday afternoon Parker had come to her with a list of questions about the Master CC&R's. She had answered the ones she could, and then, swamped with her own work, had suggested that Parker just call Jeremy himself. And now the little shit was joining them for lunch. That he hadn't told Natalie about it indicated that he knew he had overstepped his position. Natalie hastily downed two aspirin as Jeremy studied the menu.

"I'm glad you brought him onto the project," said Jeremy. "He sounds very bright."

"He is."

Parker joined them just then, apologizing sincerely but not too much, for being late. Natalie made the official introductions, since Parker and Jeremy had only talked by phone. Both men said how pleased they were to meet face to face.

Natalie's aspirin hadn't kicked in yet and her head began to throb in time to the waves of noise in the room.

Their talk focused on Bridge Creek. Parker Sherman took an active part in the conversation, coached unobtrusively by Natalie, who was put in the awkward position of having to present a united front to their client.

When their food was served, Parker and Jeremy

began a conversation about restaurants. Both of them foodies, they compared notes on their favorite spots. They joked like old pals, and Natalie noticed Parker's respectful deference to Jeremy. Underneath the easy camaraderie they were sniffing at each other like dogs.

As the men talked, one part of Natalie's mind focused on this new kink in the situation. She would have to be more cautious. And buckle down to work. She had planned to ask Parker to take a look at some documents for another project over the weekend, but now would bring them with her to Palm Springs. Annie would love that. This was supposed to have been a romantic getaway — Annie was thrilled that Natalie had come up with the idea. But then Annie had talked to Leah about it, and they'd all rented a condominium . . . Natalie couldn't let herself get off on that tangent now. Her head was splitting. She was beginning to wish she'd ordered a drink.

"I've been trying to hire this woman away from the firm for over a year now," Jeremy was telling Parker.

The first time he'd approached her, Natalie was tempted to accept his offer. She had toyed with the idea of going out on her own, developing her own small projects, and Jeremy knew that. He also knew that a few years with California Properties, his company, would give her valuable experience. But Natalie wasn't ready to give up the security she had at the firm.

"Maybe you'll come to work for me when you're ready," Jeremy said to Parker.

Natalie knew this was Jeremy's way of teasing her. She also knew that Parker Sherman didn't know enough to be helpful to Jeremy yet, and that Jeremy knew that. But it had dawned on her that she could be edged out of this situation if she wasn't careful. Parker Sherman was just the kind of person Jeremy liked on his team. A go-getter, brash and bright.

Like other developers, Jeremy Ives accepted a tremendous amount of risk. He thrived on it. If he weren't in this business, he'd be a race car driver. He played a high-stakes game of phenomenal returns or, his phrase, ball-busting losses. He palled around with entertainers and politicians. He quietly gave to his causes, often channelling the money through Natalie's firm so it wouldn't look like he was currying political favors. He had a reputation as a major behind-the-scenes kingmaker in state politics. Someone like Parker would suit him very well.

Their main courses arrived. Natalie tried to pay attention to what Jeremy was saying, but the way Parker ate distracted her.

He started with the wing of his chicken, turning it in his long, manicured fingers, looking for a point to attack. And attack he did. He tore the meat from the bones, which he then crunched into with obvious relish. He proceeded to devour his whole portion in a similar fashion. His teeth were tiny; little sharp pearls. Natalie hadn't noticed his arms until now, that appearing from each side of his white, impeccably starched cuffs was a dark mat of hair.

"You know, Natalie," Jeremy said as he cut into his fish, "I think it might be a good idea for you to bring Parker to the meeting in Riverside on Monday. That way he'd be up to speed on Bridge Creek, and if I needed you for something else, he'd be able to fill in temporarily."

Natalie swore she could hear Parker Sherman let out a silent jubilant whoop. "I'll be coming from Palm Springs, Jeremy."

"Just give him the directions. I'm sure you can work out the details between yourselves."

Between courses Jeremy excused himself to make a phone call. Natalie waited until he was out of sight before she turned to Parker.

"Why didn't you tell me you were joining us for lunch?"

Parker was cleaning his fingers on his napkin. "I didn't think it was any big deal."

He looked so innocent. This guy is really good, Natalie thought. She'd give him this round. "I just like to know these things in advance, okay?"

"No problem, Natalie." All sweetness. "I didn't mean to cause any trouble."

"You didn't, Parker. Just tell me next time."

She was going to have to pay careful attention to him from now on. She'd be able to deal with him, but she was going to have to wait until the right moment.

She managed to get home by six-thirty. She peeled off her suit and dug in the closet for jeans and a sweatshirt. She threw some clothes in the bag Annie had already packed, and was ready. Sort of. The idea of the two hour drive did not excite her. "Couldn't we just tell them I've got too much work?"

"No. Because then we'll end up staying home and you'll go to the office and that'll be the end of our long weekend."

"We could just hang out here by the pool . . ."

"Nice try, counselor, but it never works that way," Annie reminded her as they packed the car.

Natalie slid their bag into the trunk, laid their tennis racquets next to it. "I don't relish the thought of spending a weekend around newlyweds."

"They're not newlyweds. They don't even live together."

"You know what I mean. All that sexual energy makes me nervous."

Annie smiled and said, "Just quit crabbing and get in the car."

Natalie regretted griping at Annie. She was upset about Parker Sherman. She didn't really mind that they were going to Palm Springs for the weekend. Or even that Leah and her date would be there. Sometimes she put up a fuss because it was expected of her. Annie's part was to calm her down. They switched roles every so often. Tonight, though — lately — they did everything by rote. Their usual playfulness was absent from their lives. Or maybe it was just that Natalie had lost her sense of humor. Although with Maggie . . .

She dismissed the thought. She had promised herself this would be Annie's weekend and it was not off to an auspicious start.

Annie's face was lit only by headlights from oncoming cars. Natalie liked seeing her lover in this dim light. It was almost like watching a stranger. Natalie didn't know if she was registering what she was actually seeing or what she knew was there: the tiny scar at Annie's temple, mark of some childhood accident; the high cheekbones, delicate mouth.

In contrast to her lover's lightness — light brown

hair and pale blue eyes, soft pale skin — Natalie felt coarse and thick, huge. She was dark where Annie was fair. Olive complected, with dark hair and eyes. She was only a few inches taller than Annie, but was much bigger, sturdier.

Annie was the fairest of all the women she'd been attracted to. She'd never had a fascination for blondes, who to her always seemed sort of washed out. She liked her women more exotic. Normally, she wouldn't have looked twice at Maggie.

Annie glanced into the rear view mirror and caught Natalie staring at her. "What?"

"Nothing." Natalie closed her eyes. "Let's just keep driving, okay? Don't stop in Palm Springs. Don't stop anywhere."

Annie took Natalie's hand and kissed it before placing it on her thigh, where it used to belong.

Leah and Hildy had driven down earlier in the afternoon, and greeted Natalie and Annie with margaritas when they arrived.

Once, when visiting Annie at work, Natalie peeked into a room and said hello to Leah, who was sitting at an editing console, surrounded by racks of machines and monitors. "How do you know that what you punch in here," pointing to the keyboard, "is going to end up there?" Natalie had indicated the screen.

"My job's an act of faith," Leah had replied. "Every time I push one of these buttons, I have to trust that what I want to happen is going to happen. It's not like cutting film, where you actually handle the pieces. Everything is inside this box." Leah patted a machine labelled Convergence 204. "I have to believe that."

Maybe Leah carried that trust too far in her relationships. Natalie and Annie had been through quite a succession of her lovers. Like Blair, she was always dating someone. Unlike Blair, she always thought this woman was going to be the one she married. Leah was constantly working on her relationships — she spent more money on therapy, self-help books, and workshops than anyone they knew — and was always ultimately disappointed or broken-hearted when they ended.

Natalie didn't think this affair would last long. She had met Hildy a few times before and found her cute but immature.

The four women had rented a two-bedroom condo in a quiet complex a few minutes' walk from the center of town. In addition to the big main pool and jacuzzi on the grounds, their condo had its own jacuzzi.

"If I'd known how private this was, I wouldn't have bothered to pack my bathing suit," Hildy said brightly.

"Honey . . ." Leah sounded a little embarrassed.

After a brief tour of the condo, Natalie and Annie unpacked what little clothing they'd brought, then joined Leah and Hildy in the jacuzzi.

No one stayed in very long. Annie was tired from the drive, and the hot water stung Leah and Hildy's newly acquired sunburns. They said good night to one another, and Leah and Hildy eagerly went off to their room.

"That was relaxing," Natalie said to Annie as they settled under the covers.

"I'm glad we're here," Annie whispered.

"Why are you whispering?" Natalie whispered back.

"These walls are thin. I think Hildy seems nice."

"A little young." Though probably the same age as Maggie, thought Natalie. If not older.

Natalie spooned behind Annie. Coming down here was definitely the right idea, a chance to stop worrying about Maggie and Parker. She stroked Annie's side. "We're very lucky, aren't we?"

"Uh-huh," Annie murmured. She brought Natalie's hand to her breasts, down her stomach. "Want to get luckier?"

Natalie let Annie guide her hand. Maybe they could start the weekend off right. How long had it been since they'd made love? Seeing Leah and Hildy together had been a turn-on for Natalie. She could easily imagine what they might be doing now. Natalie kept seeing Hildy's strong thighs, imagined what it might be like to lie between them . . .

Annie had turned towards her now, encouraged by her response. They moved together, an awkward tangle of arms and legs. Rote again, Natalie thought as the familiar explorations began. Even here. Ultimately it was not Annie's hands or mouth but a vision of what Hildy and Leah might be doing that pushed her to an unsatisfying orgasm.

She felt dishonest afterwards, and retreated guiltily into sleep.

She woke several times during the night. Around three she opened her eyes in the unfamiliar black and heard a muffled cry from Leah and Hildy's room, then the bed springs creaking wildly. Groans followed by delighted and unsuccessfully hushed giggles. At six-thirty she looked out to see the sun hit the tops of the mountains, turning them a fiery magenta. Finally around eight she got up and went to the pool for a swim. Afterwards, she stretched out on one of the lounge chairs, closing her eyes and tilting her head to the sun.

She thought it might be fun to stay home tonight and grill something. She could pick up some chicken or fish, prepare a simple marinade. Maybe throw an eggplant or some onions on the grill.

She always wanted to cook when she was nervous or upset. It was the only activity that pushed everything else out of her head. Timing and ingredients and last-minute improvisations allowed no room for whatever troubled her — in this case Parker Sherman and his plots and strategies. She still couldn't get over how she'd let herself get caught with her guard down. She was usually more careful than that.

She had learned the hard way to question the appearance of things. After being taught all her life that her parents loved her unconditionally, that anything she did was okay with them, she was shocked to learn that wasn't true. When she came out to them, her parents had disowned her. Any pride they'd had in her law school accomplishments (top fourth of her class, law review, job offers from all over the country) was wiped out by the disgraceful way she claimed to want to live her life. None of

Natalie's considerable debating skills could convince her parents that she knew what she was doing, that she was the same person except for one small detail that they hadn't previously known. Finally she'd given up trying to plead her case to them. She stayed away from home for a very long time (especially long for someone who had grown up loving both her parents, not understanding friends who didn't get along with their mothers or father). When she finally visited them, she stated right off that she would stay as long as they were accepting of her. If anything else surfaced, she would leave. That was the only way to make her parents understand that she meant it when she said she would rather not see them than pretend to be someone she wasn't.

After a few years, both her parents not only accepted her lifestyle, they even came to visit her and Annie once or twice a year. In many ways their relationship was better than ever, certainly more honest. And yet, deep down, Natalie knew that she had won their acceptance, but not their complete forgiveness. The discrepancy made her distrustful of surface evidence; she looked constantly for the deeper meaning.

At the time of their rejection of her, Natalie had reexamined her life. The choices she made, her decision to become a lawyer. Not that she'd ever actually decided to become a lawyer. When she was little she'd sometimes go into the office with her father and draw on legal pads he gave her and sharpen pencils for him. There had never been doubt in anyone's mind as to what she'd do after college. And certainly none in hers. But she also helped her mother in the kitchen, and learned to make lots of

Armenian dishes. She'd learned about the power of food not just to nurture but to create an atmosphere of warmth and comfort. She discovered early on her talent for translating memories into meals, revising and re-creating them the way a writer builds stories around milestones in her life. Yet it never occurred to her, as the years went by and she moved closer to law school, to ask why she shouldn't do what she wanted to do, why passion alone wasn't somehow enough to change her course.

She'd accomplished almost everything her parents had assumed she would. True, always with a slight twist — like going to law school at Berkeley instead of Harvard like her father, or practicing in Los Angeles instead of Chicago. But these were always acceptable differences.

Cooking as a career would have been an unacceptable difference. Aside from being something she would do for her husband, as her mother had told her years ago, cooking was, or could be, fun, and fun was not work. At least not the kind that counted. She could have announced she wanted to be a sculptor. But cooking did not possess the creative status or even the socially acceptable cachet of art.

So she funnelled her activities through the narrow spout of law school and bar review, eliminating all extraneous pursuits. Looking back on it now, she realized she'd always chosen the path of least resistance. Not that law school was easy, but in terms of having to answer to her parents, burying herself in law school and then review courses for the bar was easier than scooting off to Paris or some culinary institute and dealing with the repercussions at home.

The only thing she'd ever done that didn't win

her parents' immediate approval was to act on the feelings she'd had for women all her life. No one in their conservative Armenian Republican circle had ever met a homosexual (or so they thought), much less been related to one. Natalie had a hard time convincing them this wasn't something she'd picked up at school in California. She saw herself as the same person they'd raised, perhaps an improved version, since she was being absolutely true to herself for the first time in her life. And for that she was punished.

Natalie always had an image of herself living in her parents' outline, a big, very general human shape, like a police firing range target. As a child, it had been an aura around her, protecting and nurturing. Then she'd grown into it, fitting perfectly into her father's sense of humor and dedication to his work, her mother's generosity. She was almost forty years old, and wondered if she'd ever outgrow the outline completely. The outline hadn't changed, but now she wondered about the comparisons she made between her life and that of her parents.

What to her seemed the most simple and logical fact, that she loved women, was what made her life subject to undercurrents of danger. Precarious, like living on a faultline.

Not that she was militant by any means, not like some gay women who were always fighting something. On the contrary, she was always censoring herself. It made life easier. Standing in line for a movie with Annie, she resisted the urge to kiss the top of her lover's head, just casually, the kind of thing she saw straight couples do all the time. Instead, she settled for a clandestine touch, or an ambiguous squeeze of her arm.

"Honey?"

Natalie opened her eyes. Annie stood over her, blocking the sun. "I must have fallen asleep." She stretched. "Are Leah and Consuela up?"

Annie pushed her playfully. "Why can't you remember that woman's name?"

"Leah's always calling her 'honey' or 'sweetie.' I'll bet she can't remember, either. Are they up?"

"I heard giggling and rustling, but they haven't emerged yet."

"We probably won't see them all weekend."

As they walked back to the condo together, "We call each other 'honey,'" Annie said.

"That's different." Natalie brushed Annie's arm with her hand, a light, affectionate gesture.

The women spent a lazy morning in and around the pool, reading magazines, talking as they floated on rafts. At one point, Natalie looked at Hildy. "Doesn't she remind you of Joan?" she asked Annie.

"Phone Joan?"

"Yeah."

Annie cocked her head as she looked at Hildy. "Not really, but I see what you mean."

"Who's Joan?" Hildy wanted to know.

"She used to be the receptionist in my office," Natalie answered. "You remind me a little of her."

But only her posture, the way she carried herself. Joan had been very plain and quiet. It was easy to forget Joan was around. Hildy was just the opposite, energetic and flirtatious, demanding attention. Hildy talked about each article she was reading, often digressing into details about many of the stars she'd worked with. When she finally put down her magazine and took up the headphones to her Walkman, "Ah, silence at last," Natalie whispered under her breath. But instead, Hildy sang along with her tape, hands and feet beating against the lounge until she got up and danced around the chair, bopping and swaying to sounds only she could hear.

Natalie watched through partially closed lids. Hildy's movements were fluid, her body supple and toned. Natalie could discern separate muscle groups as Hildy's legs and arms flexed and relaxed.

When they went inside to make lunch, Natalie said to Annie, "Hildy's getting on my nerves. She can't sit still."

"I like watching her. I think she's sexy."

"I didn't know you were attracted to immaturity," Natalie snapped.

"It's not her immaturity that attracts me." Annie bounced her eyebrows à la Groucho Marx. When she saw Natalie's hurt response, she asked "Hey, what's going on?"

Natalie couldn't stop herself. "You've got the hots for some woman and you ask me what's going on?"

"I don't have the hots for anyone. I merely said I thought she was sexy." Annie moved closer to Natalie, softened her tone. "Hey, honey, you know you have nothing to be jealous of. Don't look so worried." With her thumb she smoothed away the line between Natalie's brows.

Natalie didn't say anything. Her self-righteous anger swelled inside her.

"Do *I* have any reason to be jealous?" Annie asked. She waited a long time before gently saying, "I'm ready to listen if you want to talk."

Natalie was so taken aback by Annie's question that she couldn't make any response. The depth of love in Annie's eyes sorely tempted Natalie to blurt out everything. Here at last was a safe place. Natalie wanted to trust it.

"I just hope you know how much I love you," Annie said tenderly before embracing her.

Natalie clung to Annie as if to save herself from drowning.

They all walked into town that afternoon. As they sat outside a café eating ice cream, Natalie watched a group of five women sitting at a nearby table. They had the wholesome, practical look of grade school teachers. They joked about how guilty they felt eating ice cream, how would they get back into their bathing suits. And how none of the guys would want to dance with them. All five had bright red sunburns, wore thin-strapped summer dresses, white or cool pastels. Natalie could smell their perfumes, an intoxicating mix of scents ranging from musky to cloyingly sweet. She was close enough to see the texture of their skin, the smooth little hairs on their arms. As she imagined how firm or soft each arm was, her eyes traveled down their bodies.

She couldn't keep her eyes off the women she

saw: Hildy sitting next to her, strangers walking down the street. Just saying the word to herself — women — conjured up not so much a picture of any particular individual but a rush of sensory images crystallized by that scene: the heady scents, those arms and bare backs, sandaled feet, soft skirts swirling around legs, hands fingering thin gold chains around fine slim necks. What had gotten into her? She felt as if some valve had been turned on in her guts and she was powerless to shut it off. She was supposed to be back at the condo working. She should have been planning her strategy for Parker Sherman. But all she could think about was women.

Back at the condo, everyone went to her room. Annie dozed and Natalie worked. Or tried to. Murmuring voices from the next room, a stifled laugh, bed springs pumping rhythmically — the slightest sound from the other side of the wall kept her mind off her work and on remembered flashes of Hildy's lithe body.

That night they went out for a late dinner. Natalie could hardly take her eyes off Hildy's mouth. She kept coming back to its flawless shape: lips not pouty, not thin, not tense or tight, but of a perfect roundness. Natalie fantasized running her tongue along them, lightly tracing their outline before prying them open. She imagined attacking, fierce and hot, hunting and eager.

Natalie let her leg accidentally rub against Hildy's under the table. Just lightly, just once. "Sorry, this is a small table," she muttered. Had she imagined it, or had she felt a quick extra pressure, a moment's hesitation before Hildy withdrew her leg? God, those lips.

Back at the condo, Annie took a jacuzzi with Hildy and Leah. Natalie declined; she didn't think she could watch any more of Hildy and Leah's underwater gropings. She was already in bed with the work she hadn't finished earlier when Annie came back inside, wrapped in her towel. "That was great. You should have joined us. Leah and Hildy are going out."

"Out?"

Annie shrugged. "They felt like dancing." She climbed into bed. The hot water had brought color to her face, and her hair was damp at the ends. She smelled slightly of chlorine. "I think I'm too relaxed to read," she said before kissing Natalie and turning off her light.

Annie fell asleep immediately and Natalie worked for a few hours. She had just turned off her light when she heard Leah and Hildy come in. Giggles. Murmured voices. The moans and cries from their room were not muffled as they had been the previous night.

"Do you think they had a better time than we did?" Natalie asked Annie as they lay in bed on Monday morning. They had the place to themselves; Leah and Hildy had left Sunday night.

"Didn't you have a good time?"

"That's not what I meant. They were always laughing and giggling. And at night I could hear them. They talked for hours." In between fucking their brains out.

"They're at a stage where they don't know that much about each other," Annie explained. "And they might not be comfortable with silence yet. Think of all the things we don't need to say to communicate with each other."

"But do you miss that?" Natalie persisted.

"What? Getting to know each other?"

"I don't know. Our early days together."

Annie shifted positions, propping herself up on one elbow so she could look at Natalie. "I'm glad we had them. But I don't necessarily want to be living them again. Do you?"

"Not even the passion part?"

"Who has time for that anymore? That first year, when we couldn't get out of bed — I mean, I had a fabulous time, but it was probably one of the least productive years of my life." Annie paused, then added: "Least productive work-wise. In terms of results on my life, it was the best."

The whole time they'd talked Annie had been absentmindedly stroking Natalie's hip and thigh. Now she traced her hand lightly down Natalie's body, resting it between her legs. Annie leaned over then and kissed her. Softly at first, gently. "Are you okay, honey?"

"Yes."

"Good." Annie kissed her again, not as gently this time.

What started out slowly became urgent. Natalie allowed herself to be drawn into a perfect black space that held only the two of them.

Afterwards, she closed her eyes to make a memory

of the moment — the sound of the sprinklers going on outside, Annie's even breathing beside her, the spicy hints of her perfume covering the last lingering trace of chlorine.

This was what she'd hoped for from the weekend. Her body felt wonderfully solid on the bed, Annie's body nestled tightly against her. She always marvelled at how much closer they lay after sex, as if the psychological closeness enabled them to break some physical barrier as well. How could she want more than this? She glanced at the clock.

Annie reached for her as if she sensed, even in sleep, her lover's attention straying. Natalie kissed the top of her head. "Shower time."

But Annie drew herself even closer. "Two more minutes."

Natalie leaned over to coax Annie out of bed but instead was persuaded to remain. "Another something to remember the weekend by," Annie said as she pulled Natalie on top of her.

She must have fallen asleep for a few minutes. Before her eyes were fully open she heard Annie singing in the shower; an eclectic medley — opening with "Chantilly Lace" and somehow arriving at *Ain't No Mountain High Enough.* Natalie smiled. Annie couldn't carry a tune to save her life.

Annie leaned seductively against the wall when Natalie stepped into the stall with her. "Hey, sailor," Annie breathed, "lookin' for a good time?"

Natalie drove the first leg of the trip back. Annie would drop her at the Bridge Creek site, then continue into the city. Natalie would have to ride home with Parker Sherman. At one point in her career she would have relished the challenge of this situation, the competition. Now she was tired and a little afraid.

Annie fell asleep after about twenty minutes, and Natalie found herself thinking about a glimpse she'd caught of herself in the mirror just before she stepped into the shower with Annie.

Accustomed to looking in her own mirror, and always when she was prepared for it, this morning she had faced a stranger. In contrast to a body that looked soft and doughy, her face, especially after two days in the sun, looked dressed, finished. Her strong, even features would age well. But the little lines etched into her face that would give it its character were now gathered around her joints, her wrists and elbows. What she had originally welcomed as signs of maturity — like her first grey hairs — were suddenly danger signals. The face she recognized, but she was unwilling to claim the body. Her skin had lost the elasticity she'd once been so proud of. Her hands had become her mother's hands, used and serviceable.

Forty is not the end of the world, she thought, I'm being irrational. Age had never been important to her before. But she'd seen someone else's body in that mirror.

A terrible screeching suddenly tore through her thoughts. A car a few hundred feet ahead of her careened out of control. In the clarity of a dream Natalie watched it recover from a spin in the far right lane only to continue to slide diagonally across all four lanes of freeway — an almost balletic movement — until it hit the center divider, skidding alongside it for several yards before coming to a halt, its dented front end peering precariously into the fast lane. Traffic was light and luckily none of the drivers around her had panicked; no one had slammed on the brakes or accelerated to get out of the way, nor had the car hit anything except the center divider. The driver and passengers seemed to be all right.

Natalie continued on, amazed at the surreal quality of the incident. One minute you're driving along the freeway, the next spinning out of control, like bumper cars at an amusement park. Or being broadsided by someone like Parker Sherman. You're on your course, living your life, and you look in the mirror and realize that you're not young anymore. That life is dangerous. And finite.

She tried to pull back the memory of the safe black place she'd been in with Annie that morning, but all she saw was a dark descent into oblivion. She could hear the waters rushing around her. She was drowning.

She felt dizzy. She was out of breath, her hands sweaty from gripping the wheel. She opened her window. If she pulled over and stopped the car, Annie would wake and want to know what was wrong. And what would Natalie say? "Nothing, dear, I just realized how close we always are to death."

She looked down at the speedometer. She was doing eighty. Well, she thought, I'm not going to die unless I continue driving like this. As she slowed, she took deep breaths, holding them for five seconds, exhaling for five seconds, inhaling again for five, counting and repeating.

Natalie tried to concentrate on the meeting for Bridge Creek. Somehow, whether or not they could design an adequate landscape plan within the proposed budget seemed unimportant. Did it really matter whether they landscaped the open spaces or settled for grass? At the meeting they'd talk about how they could phase in the installation, and whether the individual or the master homeowner's group would be responsible for the upkeep of the landscaping in the common areas. Right now she couldn't have cared less. Not even the threat of Parker Sherman fazed her.

Annie woke up. She looked around, getting her bearings. "My turn to drive?"

When Natalie got out of the car, she turned and said good-bye as if nothing unusual had happened. As if she weren't now living a life completely different from the one she'd awakened to that morning in the desert.

Chapter Five
A Blast From the Past

Blair drank her morning coffee on the terrace. Normally her time for a leisurely browse through the paper, this morning she was reviewing her presentation of the concepts for Dinnertime's new "Down Home" line of microwave frozen dinners, the culmination of five weeks of work. Meat loaf, chicken pot pies — "home cookin'" was in, and companies were rushing to fill the demand for Food Like Mother

Used To Make. She would present her work along with that of the other designers on the project, offer her opinion of how to best meet the client's design objectives. A week or two later she would know which design had been chosen. Blair almost hoped it wouldn't be hers. But that had more to do with the group product manager on this account than with the product itself.

Since Dinnertime, and its parent company, FarmFresh, were big accounts for Kaplan/Shaw, Blair had worked on several projects for them. But she had yet to work directly with Lillian Webb.

Lillian was fortyish, and attractive because she made herself so. Working from plain looks, she'd built herself an image — well-dressed and perfumed, perfectly accessorized. The right jewelry with the right outfit and the expensive haircut to accent the strong shape of her face.

Lillian was on the fast track at Dinnertime. Though she'd never worked directly with Blair, she was familiar with Blair's designs and had cornered Blair once after a presentation. Like many product managers, she was looking for her own product to develop, learning as much as she could before going out on her own. When that time came, she wanted Blair to design her packaging.

Blair knew that what Lillian really wanted was Blair. Period.

Lillian Webb's pursuit had begun at Jim Shaw's annual Labor Day party at his house in Malibu. Lillian had attended with her husband, Steven, an entertainment lawyer. They could have been the model for the hip L.A. couple, Steven in his perfect bulky and elaborately patterned sweater, Lillian in a cream-colored outfit, absolutely right for Malibu.

Blair had noticed Lillian Webb's interest immediately: glances across the room, extra effort to join conversations Blair took part in. Lillian, under the watchful and possessive eye of her husband, was too smart to approach Blair directly. But when they said goodnight, Lillian had held Blair's hand for a very long time, and said how much she looked forward to their working together and getting to know each other.

Other married women had come on to Blair. They saw their married life as a safe, sane existence stretching on forever in front of them, and just once they wanted to feel someone new — and something new. How they envied Blair her freedom. Though not on a permanent basis.

Blair wasn't interested in being part of their intrigues — helping them get back at husbands or satisfying their curiosity about sleeping with a woman or whatever their reason for pursuing her. Though she wasn't immune to a little flirtation, Blair knew from experience that married women were trouble. *Straight* married women especially. She'd avoided others and she'd avoid Lillian Webb.

She'd been successful at it, too, until this project. Lillian's sharp eye, combined with her desire to work with Blair, might make her impossible to avoid. Lillian had made a point of learning to spot the unusual colors and clean style of Blair's designs, and prided herself on recognizing them in a presentation, even though that information was not given to the client.

Well, thought Blair, she couldn't worry about that now. Determined to make the best presentation possible, she gathered her things and was almost out the door when the phone rang.

"Hi, Sis."

Paul never failed to call at the worst possible time. "I'm running late, Paul. What's wrong?"

"I'm at Mother's. She's okay, but she left a pot on the stove all night with the burner on. One of the neighbors smelled something and called me."

Blair heard rattling as Paul checked for other hazards. Constance had become increasingly forgetful in the last year. Once an avid reader, she could no longer remember what she'd read from one page to the next. Sometimes she became disoriented, and would be puzzled later to find a can opener in the bedroom, or clothes strewn around the living room. Paul had taken her to several doctors, and they all diagnosed the forgetfulness and the disorientation as early signs of Alzheimer's disease.

He came back on the line. "She left the coffee maker on, too."

"What are you going to do?"

"I shut everything off. And now I've got to get to work. Mrs. Lindeman said she'd check on her later." But Paul didn't hang up.

Blair knew what he was waiting for. "Paul, you already know what I think."

"I can't put her in a home."

"I told you I'd help pay for it." Blair steeled herself for their usual argument. "She'll be well taken care of. And she'd be better off."

Paul assumed his stance. "She doesn't need that yet."

90

"Then at least find a full-time nurse or companion."

"Blair, you know how independent she is."

Already running late, Blair didn't have the time to fight with her brother this morning. "You want to wait till she hurts herself, or burns the place down?"

"You know what I want."

"Don't ask me to see her." How many times did they have to go through this?

"She's your mother."

Blair detected a note of pleading in Paul's voice. But she'd fallen for that before, never with good results. "She made it very clear she'd fix that if she could."

"That was three years ago, Blair."

"She hasn't changed since then."

"Neither have you," Paul shot back.

Always the same battles. When she didn't speak, Paul continued. "Come on, if you don't see her soon, it could be too late. She may not recognize you later on."

"Which would be just fine with her, I'm sure."

"Don't be like that."

"Look, Paul, I've already told you what I thought you should do. So either do it, or get off my back." She hung up.

"Peter Fontana's already called twice," said Dana, the receptionist.

"Oh shit. This is not going to be my day." She was increasingly fed up with clients like Peter Fontana who proclaimed their packaging theories when they hadn't been inside a market since their mothers pushed them in their shopping carts. At their first discussion of a design he had stated flatly, "We can't use blue. It's a bad color for a package." So Blair had gone out and bought everything she could find with blue in it — including several of Peter's own products — and dumped them on the conference table at their next meeting. She won that round, but he had continued to fight her every step of production.

As she walked into the conference room to meet Lillian Webb and associates, she was smoldering over her conversation with her brother, angry at the message from Peter Fontana, in no mood for placating anyone, client or no. She gave an unusually aggressive presentation, going over ten rough package concepts in three-dimensional form, explaining the pros and cons of each design, and how they would fit into the Down Home marketing strategy. She left the clients with two recommendations, one slightly more constructive than the other. Though at that moment she didn't give a damn which they chose.

When she emerged from the meeting Dana presented her with a sheaf of messages. The people at *¡Sabroso!* were anxious. Blair needed to reassure them that the re-design was proceeding well. And Paul had called.

Back in her office, she was steeling herself to return Paul's call when Dana's voice came over the intercom: "Attention everyone, we have visitors in the house." Dana's announcement meant: A client is coming through, hide any confidential products or work. Blair put a stack of folders on top of the drawing on her board, stowed some rough concepts of a new cat food box in a cabinet. As soon as an all-clear was announced, she could get back to work.

"Knock, knock." Lillian Webb popped her head in Blair's office. "I'm glad I caught you."

Blair was surprised Dana hadn't buzzed her directly. Usually clients had to be escorted. "Come in," she said unwillingly.

"Larry was taking me back to meet someone but I asked if I could make a slight detour." Lillian entered in a not unpleasant wash of perfume, looking, as always, well put together. Her bracelets jangled efficiently, not too noisily, her make-up was skillful, her hair pulled tightly back and fastened with a bow, showing to great advantage her earrings, gold bolts of lightning. She took off her suit jacket and draped it over the extra chair.

Make yourself comfortable, Blair thought.

Lillian's attractively tight skirt made it impossible for Blair to ignore the body parading in front of her. She reminded herself of her resolution not to get involved. But this was a tricky situation — Lillian was very persistent. She walked around the room as she talked, looking at Blair's drawings, at the collection of printed packages that lined the window ledge. Blair had constructed a mini-shelf of Down Home's competition. Lillian paused to examine it as she spoke.

"I've wanted to work with you for a long time. I know which of today's packages I'm pulling for. Will you tell me if I guessed right?"

"From what you said in the meeting, you showed a good understanding of the strength and weakness of each concept. That's more important than who did it." Lillian did have a good eye and deserved to be complimented on it, but Blair wasn't about to give her any more than that. Yet.

This could turn into a dangerous game. She couldn't seal Lillian the client by encouraging Lillian the individual, no matter how appealing she was. A very fine line.

Lillian resumed her prowl, touching objects, absently running her hand along the arm of Blair's chair, continuing the movement along Blair's back and shoulders. Blair sat very still.

"My husband and I are giving a dinner party Saturday night. Perhaps you could come," Lillian asked with her back to Blair, seemingly intent on the cover of the most recent issue of *Communication Arts*. "This is strictly a social party, no business. I promise."

"I've already got plans."

"You could bring anyone you wanted."

"Sorry."

"How about after? For a nightcap?"

"I don't think so, Lillian, but thanks."

"Well, before you start work on this project, okay? We'll have a drink."

"We don't know if I'm going to be the designer on this project."

Lillian smiled knowingly. "Whatever happens, then — drinks, just you and me."

Blair acquiesced. "Fine."

For the first time since she'd entered the room, Lillian faced Blair and looked directly into her eyes. "Promise?"

"Sure."

"Just you and me." Lillian put her hand to her lips, then touched Blair's lips. "I'm going to hold you to that." Then she was gone.

Blair watched her go, admiring what she was being offered. Definitely well put together. Momentarily ignoring the sticky issues, she allowed herself the luxury of a brief fantasy about Lillian. But the nagging reminder of her message from Paul stood in the way of her enjoyment.

Blair buzzed Dana. "Did my brother say anything when he called?"

"Just to tell you everything was okay, you'd know what he meant."

She did. Constance had returned from wherever her mind had wandered and once again convinced Paul that she was just fine. He would believe it until the next incident, which would prompt the next frantic call.

Blair was not immune to her brother's urgent entreaties, but she had not forgiven Constance. Of course, her anger was directed at an alive and alert and competent opponent. Blair had never adjusted the picture of her real mother to conform with Paul's current reports. She battled the supremely organized and competent mother, not the woman who sometimes wandered away from home and forgot how to get back.

Andrew, Blair's father, had been very handsome. A successful businessman, he was always late coming home. "Daddy has very important work to do," Constance would tell Blair and Paul, as if that would explain everything: why he hadn't shown up for visiting day at school, or to pick them up after play rehearsal or team practice when he had promised to be there.

Constance, Blair figured now, had always known about her husband's affairs, that's why she had buried herself in her other activities. But she never complained. And she had stayed married to her husband for twenty-seven not particularly happy years. Not that there had been tremendous fights. Passion was not conspicuous in the family. Constance had put up with her husband because it was expected of her.

She had kept busy with volunteer work. Blair would come home from school and find her mother in the loose pale blue jacket she wore at the hospital, or in a simple dress with her docent's tag from the museum pinned above her left breast. Sometimes Constance would be wearing one of her very good suits. That meant either a lecture or a luncheon to discuss raising funds for some school or library or charity. The big house ran smoothly and efficiently, a sturdy machine requiring little maintenance, its occupants living their separate lives.

Both children had already moved out — Blair working in her first job, and Paul in law school at Stanford — when Andrew's cancer was diagnosed. The family bonded together, drawn by the magnet of his illness, everyone knowing his or her role, Constance dropping all her activities to care for her husband, Blair and Paul spending weekends with their father, who was in and out of hospitals.

During that year, Blair met Hallie.

Blair had always known she was gay, but she had never felt what she felt for Hallie. Blair tried to explain it to herself. Maybe it was the fact that they had so much in common. They were both in advertising — Hallie wrote copy at a big agency. Or that each had known since childhood she was gay: neither had dated men. But the reasons didn't matter. Nothing Blair had felt for any of her other lovers had prepared her for the perfect peace she found only in Hallie's arms.

Blair brought her lover to the hospital several times. They would laugh and joke with Andrew, or just sit at his bedside as he slept. He seemed to have gained new insight in those last months, saw things in different perspective. Faced with imminent death, he placed greater emphasis on personal rather than material satisfaction. "As long as you can provide for yourself and be happy, don't worry about what anyone else thinks," he told Blair. Though they hadn't talked about it, Blair believed her father was giving tacit approval to her lifestyle. She tried to gather the courage to come out to him in the final weeks of his illness, but too many years of silence and hiding had left her without means of communication. Her tears at his funeral expressed as much sadness and loss as regret at what she had left unsaid, that she'd never told her father she knew she was going to be happy in the life she'd chosen for herself.

After her husband's death, Constance quit all her volunteer work and started watching TV. This once independent woman now looked to Blair to help with decisions: Should she move to an apartment? Should she buy a new car? The most insignificant question became cause for a phone call or worse, an impromptu visit.

One day Constance showed up unannounced and almost caught Blair *in flagrante* with Hallie. Clearly Constance wanted to know the nature of their relationship. Needing someone to practice on, and believing that because he was young he'd be more receptive to the news, Blair decided to tell Paul first.

"Don't you think you should wait to tell Mother?" was his immediate response. "Maybe it'll pass."

Sometimes she couldn't believe they were related. "*It* isn't indigestion, Paul. *It* is who I am." She took his reaction as a warning to wait a bit longer before telling her mother. But Constance was becoming increasingly dependent. How long could Blair postpone the inevitable?

Indefinitely, if she applied for jobs out of town. She began to put together her portfolio.

And as for her relationship with Hallie, Blair found it impossible not to flirt with women. Some of these incidents caused problems.

One day on her lunch hour Blair was in an art supply store to buy a few pencils. The woman who helped her was so good looking that Blair bought an expensive new set of Rapidographs she didn't need. The woman called her that night, having gotten Blair's number from her check.

Hallie was jealous. After exhausting various defensive stances, Blair claimed she couldn't help herself. "This is how I am," she declared. Of course then Hallie wanted to talk about their Relationship. Blair hated these conversations. "There's nothing to discuss," she would say before shutting herself inside a magazine or a book. Like Constance, Hallie wanted something from Blair and Blair felt she had nothing to give.

Hallie tried to stir up the passion between them. She wanted to fight, to end up in bed as they usually did after arguing. But Blair's cool facade was unbreakable. She left Hallie no edges to grip, no toeholds for discussion.

Blair flew to L.A. and was offered the position at Kaplan/Shaw. She packed up her apartment and was in L.A. before anyone had time to adjust.

Her mother was upset — she'd come to rely on Blair's advice. Blair managed to reassure Constance that she'd be only a phone call away, that this was too good a career move for her to turn down. As for Hallie — nothing Blair said bought forgiveness.

With the money Blair's father had left her, she was able to buy her place at the beach. Between work and women, Blair didn't leave a moment of time for herself. She refused to think about Hallie. The freedom she felt away from the watchful eyes of her mother was exhilarating — no chance of surprise visits here — and she'd soon established herself in a community of women who became her family.

Her first years in L.A. were marked by emotional distance from her mother — nothing new to Blair, after years of hiding who she really was — and superficial reports of her life in L.A.

Having successfully maintained her distance for five years, Blair won an Art Director's Club award and flew to San Francisco to celebrate with her mother. In the restaurant, after Constance had toasted her, Blair figured this was as good a time as any to explain all the years of silence, to finish the sentences that had hung on the phone line between them. She told her mother she was gay.

When Constance finally spoke, it was as if she were scolding Blair for some minor infraction: "If your father were still alive this never would have happened."

"How can you say that?"

"Because it's what I believe, darling." Constance took a delicate sip of champagne before starting on her appetizer.

"I've known this for a long time, Mother. Since I was a kid."

"Don't be silly. There were always young men around."

"Those were all Paul's friends. You knew that."

Blair almost forgot her mother was there with her. She had ample time during the vast silences between Constance's sentences to carry out whole conversations with her, brilliant rebuttals to her mother's statements. None of these dialogues were ever spoken. Fighting, to Blair, had always had nothing to do with feelings or emotions — just silences so long that the matter at hand simply faded away, seemingly forgotten.

"You don't have to be that way," Constance finally said, continuing a thought begun minutes before. "You could change."

"No I couldn't."

Blair marveled at her mother's ability to maintain composure. But then she had to admit that she'd probably chosen a public place for this airing of private business for that very reason, knowing that her mother's sense of decorum would ensure avoidance of a scene. Blair was not proud of her

100

cowardice. Suddenly she heard a strange sound next to her. She looked up.

Constance was cutting into her fish, her fork delicately balanced in her left hand, knife in her right. Only the slightest tremor as she raised the bit to her mouth belied her seeming composure. Blair watched her mother pause, the morsel of fish inches from her mouth, as that sound again escaped her lips.

A choked and muffled sob. No doubt about it.

Blair was amazed. She would never forget that moment, perhaps the only one that gave her a clear sense of how deeply hurt her mother was. To reduce Constance to that state — and no matter how dignified it seemed, Blair knew the extent to which she'd been pushed to exhibit even that small amount of emotion — did not make Blair proud, no matter how sure she was of the rightness of her own position.

"How could you do this to me?" Constance said before putting the piece of fish in her mouth and chewing on it as if it were poison.

The moment was broken.

"I haven't done anything to you, Mother. We're talking about me."

The busboy cleared away their uneaten main course, efficiently whisking away their plates while the waiter dusted non-existent crumbs from the table. Throughout the service Constance remained still, one hand on the thin stem of her champagne glass, the other politely in her lap.

By the time their espresso was served the two women had sat in silence for more than twenty minutes. Blair had ample time to study the other diners, wishing she could be part of their animated conversations, their heated discussions. The head waiter stopped by their table to make sure everything had been satisfactory. "Excellent as usual, Piero," Constance replied.

"Thank you, Signora," Piero nodded decorously.

When the check came, Blair reached for it, but Constance took it first. "I said it was my treat."

"I know. I thought, under the circumstances . . ."

Constance merely kept her hand on the bill as she searched in her purse for her wallet. Her hands still trembled slightly.

They did not exchange another word from that moment until Blair went back to L.A. the next morning.

They didn't speak again for several months. "It's just a little lump in my breast," was how Constance opened their first conversation. "They've caught it early, so there's probably nothing to worry about. They're doing a biopsy first thing in the morning. I just thought you should know."

How cool and composed she sounded. Blair's anger hadn't abated, but her regret at what would always be unfinished with her father made her renew her determination to bring about some reconciliation with Constance.

She flew to San Francisco the next morning, arriving at the hospital in time to learn the biopsy showed the cyst was benign. Blair was relieved on two counts: she was glad her mother was fine, and she believed this would put things in proper perspective for Constance. What would it matter who Blair slept with? Remembering her father's easier outlook during his illness, Blair was confident as she walked into her mother's hospital room.

"I'm glad you're here," Constance said when she saw her.

And it seemed true. Constance's appearance had brightened immediately, and she motioned her daughter to the chair closest to the bed.

"I've missed you." Only after she said it did Blair realize it was true. She relaxed and congratulated herself on having done the right thing by letting time and distance take their effect. "We've got a lot of catching up to do."

They chatted pleasantly. Constance was still drowsy from her medication, and she dozed on and off. She'd open her eyes to see Blair there, smile, then drift off again. The nurse brought some clear soup. Blair helped Constance sit up to eat it.

"I'm just glad all that other business is over," Constance whispered, looking around even though they were in a private room.

"What other business?"

"You know. Women."

"That hasn't changed," Blair said, surprised.

Constance stiffened. "Even after you've seen what it's done to me?"

"You're saying it's my fault you got a lump in your breast?"

"It would have been worth it if that's what it took."

"Took for what? For me to be what you call normal? Mother, it's not going to happen."

"So you came back to make me sicker? Is that what you want?"

Constance then unleased a tirade about how disgusting Blair was, and how she was doing this deliberately, that if she really loved Constance she would change. She finished with "Just get out! Get out! You repulse me! I don't have a daughter anymore!"

Blair fled the hospital, her mother's words following her out to the street and all the way back to L.A..

The volume of her mother's accusations had grown fainter, but their effect hardly diminished three years later. Each call from her brother stirred up the memories, and Blair would fall back into the circle of anger and hurt.

With the holidays approaching, she needed to start looking for distractions to take her mind off her anger. Otherwise it would become her brightest ornament, splendid and untarnished still.

Often the holidays were a busy time at work. Clients wanted projects finished and waiting for them when they came back from their vacations. This year, however, Blair would wrap everything up just before Christmas. Everyone else at work would think her lucky. She was going to have to find something to do.

Lillian Webb offered a tempting, if dangerous, diversion. As Blair wondered if she couldn't come up with something safer, her intercom buzzed. "Roxanne Tucker for you on three-five," Dana announced.

Blair leaned to get the phone. She smiled. Maybe sometimes you were allowed to get what you needed.

Chapter Six
The Big Four-Oh

"Hear it's almost your birthday," had been Parker Sherman's subtle introduction to the topic as they stepped into the elevator that morning. He gave Natalie a lesson on this amazing salve he'd gotten from his dermatologist. Originally developed as an acne medicine, it turned out to have remarkable anti-wrinkle properties. He talked all the way to the fifteenth floor. Just the way I wanted to start my day, Natalie thought as she left him at the reception area.

Natalie didn't like being reminded of this birthday. Most of her friends waved away her apprehension — "You look younger than all of us! What are you worried about?" But Natalie felt she was no longer living up to her potential, that her potential was behind her, and she could only fear what lay ahead.

A small package sat on her desk. No tag identified either the sender or the store it came from. Natalie held the box in her hand before opening it. It was very light. She removed the plain brown paper. The next layer was shiny royal blue tied with thin ribbons of shocking and pale pink. Still no card. She neatly tore through the wrapping. The small white box had no identifying markings.

Nestled in hot pink tissue paper was a pair of earrings, large free-form shapes that reminded her of amoebae, each earring made of three pieces of some kind of metal: one silver, one black brushed with what looked like gold leaf, one with white gold. She'd only seen one other pair even remotely similar — on Maggie that night they'd had dinner. These had to be Sydney originals.

Any of her friends who saw the earrings would say they weren't suited for her. Depressing as it was to admit to herself, they'd be right. Her taste ran to classic styles, dresses and suits and slacks (although she never wore pants to the office) she could wear for years. She'd tire of an outfit long before it wore out. Not that she didn't sometimes try to break away from that and jazz up her wardrobe. But none of her attempts had ever been successful, and she was by now resigned to her conservative, traditional look.

Maggie's up-to-date clothes had influenced Natalie so much that she had gone out one afternoon and impulsively bought a jacket to wear on weekends, a funky, bulky, shoulder-padded thing. She modeled it that night, and when she saw the surprised look on Annie's face, she knew she shouldn't have bought it. "You don't like it," she'd said, dismayed.

"No, it's great," Annie said. "It's just so . . ." Here she'd paused discreetly, "Not you."

She found the note under the earrings. "Happy Birthday." It was signed simply, M. How had Maggie known it was her birthday?

Natalie turned the earrings in her hand. They were more like abstract sculpture than jewelry. Expensive, she thought. Expensive and totally inappropriate. Unless this wasn't so much a birthday present as it was a thank you for the referral to Delia Owens. Delia had told Natalie she was thinking of offering Maggie a permanent position after she finished school and passed the bar. Of course. That's how Maggie would have found out about her birthday. Delia was invited to the party, Delia must have told Maggie about it, and Maggie had used the opportunity to say thank you. The present was no more than a gesture, albeit an extravagant one.

But the question remained: What was she going to do with these earring? She tried one on. Considering their size, they were amazingly light and comfortable. She dug into her purse for a mirror. She had to angle her face away and look sideways. The silver was a good contrast against her dark hair, and the gold leaf on black provided a nice highlight between the silver and white gold. What in her hand had seemed an undefined, amoebic shape, against her face became a flattering ornament. But then this was just an earring on an ear, detached and separate from her face, her image of herself. Seeing them on anyone else, Natalie would have paid the wearer compliments. She'd expect them on someone like Blair. She tried to see her whole face in the tiny mirror, but couldn't. Not that it mattered. These weren't for her. Even if she had the nerve to wear them, how could she explain to Annie where they'd come from?

She put the earrings back in the box.

Natalie hadn't seen Laura Harper, *née* Wasserman, since college. Laura had called from Boston weeks ago to say she was coming to L.A. on a business trip with her husband and wanted to see Natalie. Natalie couldn't for the life of her remember what had possessed her to agree. She had been in a meeting when the call came in, and it had been easier to say yes than come up with an excuse — a decision she immediately regretted.

Laura was one of the few straight people Natalie had come out to in college. The strain of secrecy had made Natalie withdraw from her other straight friends and suspend her activity with campus anti-war groups. She had spent most of her time with her lover and a small, closeted circle of gay women.

In the years immediately after college and law school, when some of her friends were most eager to continue their relationships, Natalie took subtle and not so subtle pains to discourage any intimacy. It was simply easier not to see people than to use up all her energy avoiding questions such as where — with its underlying subtext with whom — she had spent a holiday weekend, or the more blunt so who are you seeing these days. Her school friends reached towards her, making the effort to stay in touch, offering to keep their schedules clear to accommodate her busy one. Sometimes she'd make a date with them only to cancel at the last minute. Sometimes she'd spend an awkward hour or so chatting about nothing in particular, avoiding any real conversation for fear of having to tell her story. She could sense their bafflement at her distance. Eventually they'd stopped calling. A few still sent cards.

Laura had kept in touch over the years with newsy letters each Christmas, along with an occasional photo of the boys. In college, Laura had been known as the Cheerleader of the New Left because she dated all the campus radicals and was passionately involved in their causes. She surprised all her friends when, shortly after graduation, she married Cameron Harper, a law student who hadn't been involved in any of their protest groups. Then astounded them even more by having her first of two sons before the year was up. Her college buddies all saw this as the supreme cop-out. In their eyes, Laura had sacrificed her potential to her husband's career. She'd thrown away all her valid causes and settled instead for the life they'd sworn to avoid, that of their mothers.

Far from sounding unhappy, Laura's letters to Natalie were filled with the contented drone of family life.

What a shame, Natalie thought as she parked down the street from the restaurant. Still, she was surprised to feel a little apprehensive about seeing

Laura. They'd been out of school almost twenty years now, and comparisons were inevitable, if only physical ones. Laura was probably one of those tennis-playing housewives who radiated good health and an affluent lifestyle.

Might as well get it over with. She tilted the rear view mirror towards her then took off her prim diamond studs and replaced them with the earrings Maggie had given her. This might be her only chance to wear them.

If she hadn't walked into the restaurant looking for Laura, Natalie wasn't sure she would have recognized her. But, "Look at you, you haven't changed a bit!" Laura gushed. "Well, maybe a little grayer, but who isn't? It's so good to see you."

Natalie mumbled something appropriate before burying herself in the menu, using it as a shield while she adjusted to the shock of seeing her friend. This had nothing to do with their different lifestyles and everything to do with Laura's appearance.

"You know who else lives out here now?" Laura asked while Natalie studied the menu. "Franny Dwight. She's somewhere near the beach. Do you ever run into her?"

Natalie answered yes and no as each question required, hoping her face didn't give away her thoughts.

Laura had gained fifteen or twenty pounds since college. But it was age that obscured her features; Laura's face looked softer, less defined, as if Laura were disappearing before Natalie's eyes and a middle-aged matron were taking over.

Natalie had been prepared to endure lunch, to suffer through stories about the boys and Cam,

110

vacations and emergency trips to the vet — an in-person version of Laura's newsy family-oriented letters. Instead she was presented with photographs of two young men, a brief history of Laura's going back to school for her master's degree and her new involvement in a literacy program. Natalie's own life, in contrast, seemed to have been blown off course. Faced as never before with everything she could have done, the realization made her head spin. She only half-heard Laura's glowing reports of Ben's early acceptance to Penn, Cam Jr.'s first year at Vassar. Though not deliberately, Laura was making an excellent case for the choices she'd made in her life.

Natalie and Annie had discussed the idea of having a baby, or adopting one, eventually coming to the conclusion that they were too old, didn't have the patience — Natalie couldn't even remember the excuses they'd given. Maybe they'd just been too scared. Whatever, Natalie now faced the emptiness and finality of their decision. All her achievements seemed as nothing compared to what Laura had done. Missed opportunities shouted at her from the void of her life. What had she been doing all these years?

"Excuse me," she blurted, standing up so quickly she almost knocked over her chair. Her heart pounded; she felt light-headed.

Laura half rose to help Natalie. "Are you all right?"

"Fine. I'll be right back."

In the ladies' room, Natalie braced herself against the cool porcelain sink. Head bowed, unable to face the mirror, she let cold water run over her wrists. She wet a towel and drew it over her neck, across her forehead. She pressed it against her eyes.

She'd had a modest fantasy once, not earth-shattering, not particularly socially redeeming, but something that had entered her mind and never quite escaped. She had wanted to re-create on a larger scale intimate dinners with her family, to be able to foster an atmosphere of warmth, discussion, nurturing. She wondered now how her life would have turned out if she'd followed that impulse.

She had previously judged the choices Laura had made and found them lacking. Again she asked herself what was wrong with doing something you were good at, liked to do, and, in the case of cooking, gave other people pleasure? How could you judge a life? And who had set her up as judge, anyway? She could only be responsible for herself. The accumulation of evidence showed she maybe hadn't even done such a good job at that.

When her pulse subsided she returned to the table. A gulf now stretched between her and Laura. Laura looked worried. Was Natalie okay? Natalie withdrew from Laura's concern, unable to respond honestly, ashamed at her jealousy. She ached for what might have been and what now seemed totally beyond her reach. "I'm fine, really," she said, eager to move on to safer ground, the kind of conversation she'd imagined they'd have.

Natalie drove Laura back to her hotel. Laura urged Natalie to come to visit them in Boston. "I'd love to meet Annie, and I want you to meet my family." Laura reached across the seat to hug Natalie, an awkward but sincere embrace.

• • • • •

Back in her office, Natalie couldn't settle in to work. She got up once to get herself coffee (not even decaf, hoping the unaccustomed afternoon buzz would encourage productivity), again to meander into the library to check on a case precedent. She returned all her phone calls. She even walked down the hall to Parker Sherman's office to ask for his dermatologist's number. She spread out her papers on Bridge Creek but couldn't concentrate. She couldn't escape the sense of loss, of having missed out.

She realized with a start that she was still wearing Maggie's earrings. She took them off and changed back into her studs. A blast of guilt when she remembered Maggie — and it wasn't just an image of Maggie, detached, but Maggie in the kitchen, Maggie's look, Natalie's impulsive move to her, stepping forward and grabbing her in one motion. She heard again Maggie's barely audible sigh when they kissed, felt the soft flannel shirt Maggie had worn under the judge's robes, that first exquisite touch of bare skin.

Somewhere along the line she'd messed up. She longed for some definitive way to measure her life. She would even settle for a glimmer of hope for a promising future, like the one Maggie had ahead of her. The dangerous nature of her thoughts convinced Natalie that work was the safest place now. She tucked the earrings away in the back of a desk drawer and returned to the intricate details of the practice of real estate law.

Coordinating all the aspects of a development like Bridge Creek was a bear. No matter how much time she devoted to the task, there was always more work to be done, even with Parker Sherman doing a lot of the tedium. And that thought brought its own problems. She could hear the scuffle of Parker's expensive loafers behind her, feel his eager breath on the back of her neck. She worked on into the evening.

She jumped when her private line rang. Without looking up from the page she was working on, she activated the speaker phone. "I'm practically out the door," she said.

Annie's silence suggested she knew better.

Natalie looked at her watch. "Twenty minutes."

"You're leaving in twenty minutes or you've got twenty minutes of work left to do?"

"I'll be home in time for *L.A. Law.* But in case I'm not . . ."

"I know. Tape it."

She went into the bathroom and splashed cold water on her face. She studied her image.

Ever since the weekend in Palm Springs she'd made a point of peering into mirrors, trying to catch a glimpse of the stranger she'd seen that morning in the desert. Without the element of surprise, however, she was faced always with herself, or the person she'd come to recognize as herself. With only one major difference: she couldn't look in a mirror, no matter how fleeting the glance, without thinking about her own death. Trite as it seemed, all the information came simultaneously: your hair looks fine and one day you're going to die. And earlier, when she'd finally faced herself in the restaurant, came the added, What kind of legacy are you going to leave behind? Bridge Creek and a string of mini-malls?

She leaned forward, turning her head to the side. Dark circles underscored her eyes. Just the fluorescent light, or the result of having been in the office since eight-thirty that morning after working late the night before? But what about the little lines around her mouth? They were new. Or was she just noticing them for the first time?

As she rode down in the elevator she reconsidered Parker's lecture on the benefits of vitamin A cream.

Only the outside lights and a dim light on a timer in the living room were visible when she pulled the car into the garage. She walked straight through to the bedroom, making sure on her way that the French doors onto the patio were locked, the windows secured. "Honey, I'm home!" she called out in her best Ricky Ricardo imitation.

Annie was sitting up in bed watching television and doing a crossword puzzle. Natalie kissed the top of her head, then started to undress.

"How'd your lunch go?" Annie asked.

"Fine. She did most of the talking. You know, family stuff." Natalie gave a brief and much-edited version of their conversation, omitting all her reactions. "Her sons are grown. It's amazing. Where does the time go?" Tony barked to be let in, and Natalie crossed the room to open the door.

"Well, some things never change," Annie said. "I had a long talk with Leah today. She can't decide whether to break up with Hildy."

Natalie climbed into bed, settled back against the pillows. "The saga continues."

"Don't be snide. It would be nice if she could settle down with someone."

They watched the last half hour of *L.A. Law*. It and the news that followed served as little more than white noise for her, a futile attempt to eliminate the day from her head and ready herself for sleep. Natalie jotted a few notes about Bridge Creek on a pad she kept by the bed. Once she spoke into the microcassette recorder never out of arm's reach. And she kept thinking about babies. The idea that maybe that's what was missing floated above her thoughts. She even had a crazy notion that maybe with Maggie . . . Too keyed up to sleep and too tired to read, she lay in the dark, willing herself to relax.

She repeated this routine every night. If she did manage to sleep, she'd wake with a vague sense that something was wrong, get out of bed, and with Tony at her side, check all the doors and windows. Often she'd end up sitting at the dining table looking out at the darkness, feeling something looming over her.

When they'd first moved into the house, they were enchanted by the location. About three-quarters of the way up the canyon, it was set near the front of a lot that butted up against the side of the hill. Natalie loved the thought that deer wandered across their backyard — "If you could call anything that steep a back yard," she always said. A low retaining wall cut into the hill, carving enough room behind the house for a jacuzzi, swimming pool, and surrounding patio.

116

The hillside was heavily planted with shrubs and vines — jasmine, lantana, pyracantha, bamboo — and the house was surrounded by trees. "It's going to feel like being on vacation all the time!" Annie had exclaimed when they decided to buy it. Even the air was different, fragrant with fresh smells of wild grasses and sage.

They had to make some concessions, however. They lost two cats to the coyotes before they bought Tony. And sometimes during the rains they were stuck at home because the road became impassable. The majority of the time, however, they had nestled happily against the protecting shoulder of the hillside.

But lately, especially at night, the hill seemed bigger and more forbidding. Instead of feeling they lived in its shelter, Natalie saw herself in its shadow. Sitting up through the nights, she felt an urgent need to break out before that silent chunk of canyon crushed the house. Events like that actually could happen in the rains, and Natalie became convinced that they were only one big storm away from disaster.

Natalie took off the afternoon before her birthday to prepare for the party the next night. She was poaching a salmon while she gathered the ingredients for gumbo. The sky had been grey and threatening all day, the radio said a major storm front would be moving into the area. Natalie didn't even have to look out the window to know it was coming: shadows on the wall danced and whirred; she sensed movement out of the corner of her eye. Outside, leaves shimmered and shook, the air was alive with sounds. Wind in the trees, whistling under the door, rattling windows in their casings. A brass bell hanging from a tree clanged constantly, its usually sweet chimes whipped into urgent alarm.

Around five she went outside to close the umbrella on the patio table. The wind gusted so fiercely Tony wouldn't follow her, merely stood in the doorway watching. Already leaves and pine needles littered the area and swirled around her or blew into the pool. The tang of eucalyptus and cedar seasoned the air.

Natalie arched her neck to look up at the huge palm closest to the house. It swayed pliantly in the wind. Would it survive another storm? She wished she'd had the gardener out to do something about it. She eyed it suspiciously before going back inside.

All her nocturnal fears gathered with the storm. She'd been looking forward to cooking, her best relaxation technique. But now even that didn't soothe her. She worked steadily, browning chicken, making the roux for her gumbo and adding it to the stock. She cooked all evening and as she cooked she worried.

As predicted, the huge electrical storm moved through the canyon, the rain starting while she was cooking, hurled against the windows and doors by gusts of wind. She knew the panic rising in her would disappear with the storm. That the next night, her birthday, they'd be celebrating and the house would be filled with friends. She'd be fine then, she kept telling herself.

She and Annie ate dinner watching the news. A brief lull in the story made her hopeful that the worst was over. But that night she awakened when deeply echoing thunder entered her dream. At first she thought it was an earthquake. Tony was so scared he kept trying to climb into bed with them. Unable to get back to sleep, and not wanting to disturb Annie, she took Tony with her into the living room and stretched out on the couch. Rain hammered the roof and thunder blasted. Palm fronds sailed past the window. The wind scraped leaves along the terrace, blew down through the chimney and into the room. It knocked at the windows, demanding entry.

Lightning ripped the sky and she watched the room strobe from night to day and back again. Water gushed over the sides of the gutters on the roof, flowed out of the downspouts like fountains. She fell into a semi-sleep, uneasy and filled with violent dreams.

An explosive crack jolted her awake. The palm! No, she realized, sitting up, heart slamming in her chest, one of the french doors had blown open. It banged shut, only to be flung wide by the next gust. Natalie rushed to get towels to absorb the water. Tony cowered nearby. She lashed the door with wire to hold it in place. As she mopped up the water, she remembered the aftermath of past storms, whole trees floating down the shallow river that just hours earlier had been the road in front of their house. Again she imagined the hillside shifting suddenly, sliding, then crashing into the house, shattering through the french doors . . .

She poured herself a drink. She stood at the doors and peered out into the night.

The wind had stopped. She could see the rain in the lights, falling as if weighted. It bounced off each surface, outlining everything with an aureole of water. The patio furniture sat patiently enduring the downpour. The black cover of the barbecue gleamed, washed clean. The pool was close to overflowing, leaves matted on the wet decking. Natalie was surprised to see that except for the scattered leaves and branches and one large potted azalea that had blown over, everything looked the same as usual.

Everything safe again. Or still. Yet how precarious everything seemed. What if something had happened? They were always so complacent, never thinking anything could go wrong. But their lives could change in a split second.

"Nat?" Annie's sleepy voice called from the bedroom.

She went to Annie's side of the bed. "I didn't want to wake you."

"Who could sleep through that?" Annie pulled back the covers and made room for her. "Were you working?"

"I fixed the latch on the french doors." She climbed into bed.

Annie lazily ran her hands along Natalie's body. "Happy birthday, honey," she whispered before settling back to sleep.

Not trusting the calm, Natalie maintained her vigil under the now gentle and steady drumming of the rain.

The morning dawned clear and beautiful. Except for the dark wet tree trunks and scattered leaves and small branches, the house and yard seemed to have forgotten the rain. The palm tree she'd been so worried about stretched to the brilliant blue sky. In the light of day the hill was innocent, marvelously green, with a bright patch of fuchsia bougainvillaea igniting one whole upper corner. The sparkling day helped her to forget the violence of the storm and her moment of panic. The brightness even embarrassed her a little.

Annie disappeared for a minute, returning with two huge bags full of presents and cards and singing *Happy, Happy Birthday Baby* (or, with her singing ability, the closest thing to it). As always, there were cards from Annie, from Tony, from "A Secret Admirer." They ranged from playful and sexual to corny and serious. The presents were elaborately wrapped. Annie and Natalie had always made a big deal of special occasions, birthdays, and anniversaries.

Natalie started in on the smaller packages first. Several hardback volumes of Dickens (Annie was buying her the complete works, a few at a time), two Patricia Highsmith mysteries she hadn't read. Next she unwrapped an eclectic mix of CD's. "These are great," Natalie said.

She hoped she was being appropriately appreciative. By now Annie knew that Natalie was not effusive, that showing enthusiasm was hard for her sometimes. But with each present Natalie felt a greater burden, a stronger sense that nothing was right.

"Now for the *pièce de résistance*," Annie announced with a flourish, pulling a tiny box out of the shopping bag.

The small box from Tiffany's contained a pair of gold and lapis earrings. They were gorgeous. They were also neat, tidy, and classic. Just like every other pair of earrings she wore with one secret exception. To avoid having to say anything, Natalie just hugged Annie.

"I hope you like them."

"How could I not?" Natalie said, still holding Annie.

Natalie let Tony out and threw a tennis ball for him. He scrambled up the hill, coming back with the ball and a nice branch, panting and all smiles. Natalie hosed the patio, clearing the debris washed down by the rain, the nozzle throwing out rainbows with the spray. She and Annie dried off the table and chairs and ate a late breakfast outside.

Annie disappeared into the house, returning a moment later with a box wrapped in bright paper and tied with several colors of ribbon.

"More?" Natalie asked, genuinely surprised.

"How many times do you turn forty?"

"Only once, God willing."

Inside the package was a guidebook to Paris. Natalie looked at Annie. "You didn't . . ." Annie smiled expectantly as Natalie tore open the envelope. Two airline tickets to Paris. Natalie was speechless.

"I couldn't think of a better place to celebrate," Annie said.

Natalie thumbed through the guidebook, feeling Annie's eyes on her, anxiously waiting for her reaction. Wanting desperately to respond appropriately, to seem excited, Natalie was again aware of the improper fit of this day. "I don't know when I can get away . . ." Knowing that was the wrong response.

"The tickets are open-ended," Annie said. "I knew if I didn't get them we'd never go."

"That was smart." Wrong again.

Annie looked at her, puzzled.

"What?" Natalie asked. As if she didn't know. But was just stalling for time.

"I guess I thought you'd be more excited."

"I am excited, honey. I just don't know what to say."

Annie grinned. "Thank you would do fine."

"That wouldn't be enough." Natalie was still in shock.

Believing that action was better than words, she drew Annie to one of the chaises in the sun. She unbuttoned Annie's shirt, nestled closer to her, burying her head between her lover's breasts.

Annie pulled Natalie's head back. "Are you okay?"

Natalie nuzzled closer.

"Is that an answer?" Annie wanted to know.

"It's a question," said Natalie.

Which Annie answered by placing her hands on Natalie's head and guiding it down her body. Natalie knelt by the chaise and let Annie direct her. She tried to concentrate on what she was doing, nibbling the smooth skin of Annie's belly, but the ground was very hard. "My knees are killing me," she said.

"Come up here, then," Annie said.

Natalie balanced awkwardly on the chaise. The frame dug into her back.

Seeing her discomfort, Annie shifted position. "Is that better?"

Natalie's left arm was now pinned underneath her. "Not really." She took Annie's hand and they went into the bedroom.

"There was a time we would have figured it out on the chaise," Annie said.

"Some of us are older now. We've grown used to our little comforts."

"Enough of this 'old' shit. Come here." Annie pulled Natalie to her.

The phone interrupted their kiss.

"Leave it," Annie pleaded, working her hands into Natalie's jeans. "Just this once."

But Natalie already had the receiver to her ear.

"Natalie, hate to disturb your Saturday . . ."

"No problem, Jeremy," she said. She had the information he needed in her briefcase which was in the den. She put him on hold so she could change phones. Annie was in the shower by the time Natalie came back.

They spent the rest of the day getting ready for the party.

Finally everything was done and all Natalie had left to do was fix her hair and put on her new gold and lapis earrings. Annie came up behind her as she stood before the mirror, placing her hands on Natalie's hips and pressing into her, murmuring "Let's finish what we started this morning."

"They'll be here any minute," Natalie said, running a brush through her hair.

Annie buried her face in Natalie's neck. "You smell so good," she whispered, eyes closed. She stood that way a moment, her hands beginning to explore Natalie's body. "I wish we could leave for Paris right now." She sighed and pushed herself away from Natalie. Another quick kiss and she was off.

Natalie thought of Paris. City of Lights. She imagined waking up in a small hotel on the Left Bank. Breakfast of croissants and *café au lait* before going back to bed — a flash so vivid she could feel the coarse clean white sheets. But it was Maggie she saw lying there next to her, not Annie.

Natalie faced the mirror again. As she fastened her earrings the angle of her head highlighted her grey streak. Her make-up masked the network of tiny lines she'd recently discovered. Natalie looked at herself. Nothing she did, no tricks with foundation or mascara could cover the almost familiar face she saw staring back at her. Her own deceit showed through every layer of make-up. How much longer before it was visible to others?

She dreaded this party because she knew what would be expected of her. She was the one her friends turned to on birthdays, holidays, at any large gathering. They looked to her to speak, to sum up the occasion, to bestow an appropriate significance on the event, to provide an instant analysis that defined their lives. Her life with Annie, her marriage to Annie, was an example to them. She and Annie had become living proof of the possibilities of happiness through commitment. A part of the community giving greater meaning to the whole.

The doorbell rang. Footsteps followed by muffled sounds of greetings. She heard the voices move into the living room. Laughter. Then Tess's voice booming down the hall. "Where's the birthday girl? I want to give her a hug."

Natalie hadn't turned from her reflection. "Liar," she said to the woman in the mirror. "Big forty-year-old liar."

The center of attention at the party was a photo collage that Annie and Blair had put together as a surprise for Natalie. Mounted on two huge boards were snapshots of her and her friends, a record of the last ten years of her life, with the addition of a bunch of baby pictures Annie had culled from a huge stack Natalie's mother had sent.

Most of the pictures were of Annie and Natalie together: the summer they had traveled in Europe; with friends lying by the pool; at parties; at their commitment ceremony. Some images embodied a period of time: the year they bought this house, the year they brought Tony home as a puppy, the year she was made a partner in the firm. The photographs held only smiling eyes frozen by the camera.

The most recent batch of prints had been taken at the Halloween party. There was one of Natalie with Maggie, Tess, and Blair, Natalie the hippy making a peace sign with each hand. Natalie tried to determine if the shot had been taken before or after the kiss in the kitchen. But what signs could she look for? She carried no visible traces of that moment.

"Feel like your whole life is passing before your eyes?" Irene Fields, working on her second portion of gumbo, stood next to Natalie.

"How'd you know?"

"I turned forty a few years ago, remember? Don't worry, you get over it. Plus, you'll never look your age."

"Is that your professional opinion?" In addition to being Natalie's longtime friend, Irene was her doctor.

Irene nodded. "I guarantee it." She took another bite of gumbo. "Not only do you look good, but you sure can cook."

Despite the playful banter with Irene, Natalie was plagued by morbid thoughts. Time was moving inexorably forward. Not hurtling, no, but slow and deliberate and she was acutely aware of its passage and powerless to stop it. When she was a child, she'd been fascinated by the sweep of the second hand of her father's watch, aware with each tick that that moment was gone, never to return. That moment, and this one. And this one.

She had reached the age of regular mammograms, of being frighteningly aware of every lump and bump. Her joking relationship with Irene could change drastically, Irene becoming the bearer of bad tidings, then caring for her during a long and fatal illness.

All this morbid fantasy touched off by Irene Field's reassurance that she looked great for forty.

All around her, everyone was having a great time. The party was a huge success, with Natalie the impostor locked safely inside its center.

All her fears were shut in with her. Age scared her. So did mirrors. The memory of a few wild and unpredictable seconds in her kitchen frightened her.

Suddenly the lights went out and everyone started singing happy birthday. Natalie was surrounded by a circle of her friends, women she considered family.

Coming towards her was Annie, carrying the cake topped with lit candles. The light from the tiny flames illuminated Annie's smiling, proud face as she approached.

Natalie looked at Annie and felt a rush. She saw an attractive stranger, someone with her mysteries intact, all her sharp edges not yet worn down by compromise and the constant give and take that goes with any marriage. She felt that same jolt she had when she saw Annie for the very first time.

If she could have, Natalie would have sent everyone home at that moment and sat down and told Annie about everything: her strange thoughts, her need to know she made some difference in the world. Her fear of mirrors. And of Maggie.

When she blew out the candles, the lights came back on, and with them Annie's familiarity. Annie involved in the business of cutting and distributing slices of cake. Natalie was left with her dark insecurity, not knowing how close she was to flashpoint, knowing only that the slightest misstep could trigger an explosion.

Chapter Seven
Time Zones

Blair enjoyed herself at Natalie's party, relaxed in the safe atmosphere around her friends. Neither Paul nor Lillian could intrude here. When everyone called on Natalie to make a speech, Natalie pleaded shyness.

"Since when?" Tess shot back, and everyone laughed.

Natalie seemed unusually reluctant to speak. Casting several imploring glances toward Annie, even a stray one at Blair, Natalie moved slowly to the front of the group gathered to celebrate with her.

"I'm too old for speeches." But her audience wouldn't let her get away without at least a few words. So Natalie held her glass high in a toast to Annie and to their guests and thanked them all for the presents and for the party. "And you'd better enjoy it," she warned, "because I'm not planning on having any more birthdays. Ever." Everyone laughed and applauded.

Blair was surprised at the brevity of Natalie's toast. Tonight, Natalie was not being a spokeswoman for any cause. Just as well, thought Blair. All that relevance can get tiresome.

She joined Natalie at a table with six other women happily eating cake and drinking coffee. Tess was about to leave for her annual pilgrimage to see her mother in Florida, to regale her with stories about her work and how much money she was making, always keeping silent about her social life.

Sandy, chiropractor to most of the women in the room, said, "You have to come out to your mother, Tess. How can you have an honest relationship with her otherwise?"

Blair didn't subscribe to that theory anymore. And she agreed with Tess, who said, "I'll tell her one day. Timing is all. Remember DisneyWorld."

She referred to when she had once broached the subject, tactfully picking up on the topic of the day on Phil Donahue: gays and their families. Since her mother had done very well with the introductory talk about lesbians and gay men, Tess resolved to bring up the punch line — her being gay — at the earliest opportunity. They went to DisneyWorld the next day.

Walking through Fantasyland, Tess's mother stopped dead in her tracks to stare at two very hard-core dykes who walked by. She pointed at them and eagerly tugged Tess's arm. "Get a look at that! There's two of them leprechauns you were telling me about!"

The conclusion Tess drew from this exclamation was that her mother was clearly not ready to hear Tess's news.

"She may never be ready," Sandy said. "You still have to tell her."

Not everyone was as militant as Sandy. Jenny, her lover, argued the other side. "Her mother lives three thousand miles away, they get along, why ruin a good thing?"

Nicole and Emma, both therapists, jumped in. They were in favor of being as open as possible, admitting that sometimes it wasn't in everyone's best interest to come out to their families. Tess was no longer paying attention to the brouhaha she'd started. She was wallowing in the adoring gaze of Sarah, basking in the sexual glow of her new relationship. The two of them were always touching, a hand on the other's thigh or shoulder. Tess would reach towards Sarah's breast only to have her hand deflected by a modest Sarah. When Sarah left the table to get more food, Tess leaned in and confided to the table, "I think I'm in love!"

Like all new converts to a religion or cause, Tess couldn't stay away from the topic of her conversion. "As long as I've got two authorities at the same table —" She looked to Blair and Natalie. "Maybe we can answer this question: How do you decide your anniversary? Is it the day you meet, the first time you sleep together, or the moment you realize you're in love?"

"Are we assuming this all doesn't happen the same night?" Blair asked, only half joking.

"Don't look at me," Natalie demurred. "I'm not such an expert."

"Are you kidding? You've been married for ten years." Tess turned to Sarah. "Why don't we get married?"

Tess reached for Sarah under the table. Blair noticed an attractive blush spread across Sarah's face.

Tess, once again more involved in Sarah than the conversation, didn't seem to care that Natalie didn't answer her question. But the rest of the group had no trouble switching from the politics of coming out to the politics of relationships. Leah, always delighted to talk about her favorite topic, had joined the discussion, which soon expanded to include how long — or briefly — relationships lasted in the community. "I wish I could stay with someone for more than six months," Leah sighed.

"That's my point exactly," exclaimed Nicole. "We're not encouraged to stay together." She was an intense, curly haired woman who had been involved in gay rights struggles since the seventies. "The law doesn't support us, society doesn't support us, and God knows most of our families don't. We're in relationships sanctioned by no one but ourselves. We don't have traditions or ceremonies of our own. That's why relationships like Annie and Natalie's are so important to our community."

"What are you saying? Let's play straight America and get married? We should be able to do better than that." Blair said this more to get a rise out of

Natalie than to be involved in the discussion. But Natalie wasn't biting.

Nicole was. "But why? It's not the institution that needs changing, it's the way people commit themselves to it. That's why Natalie and Annie's wedding was a political statement."

Blair thought she saw Natalie cringe at that. "I wouldn't go that far," she said. "We just wanted to state publicly that we were building a life together."

Not the kind of rousing commentary Natalie usually gave. This was her kind of discussion, and she seemed a million miles away.

"Well," Nicole said, "it was your wedding. But some people saw it as more symbolic than that."

Emma supported her lover's argument. "You did what a lot of us are too afraid to do. It was —"

"An affirmation of our own relationships," Nicole concluded, rounding out Emma's thoughts.

At that point Natalie excused herself to take a stack of dishes into the kitchen.

"What's wrong with her?" Tess wondered out loud.

"Modest, I guess," Blair said, but she, too, had been struck by Natalie's discomfort with the topic.

Blair flashed back to Halloween. She hadn't given much thought to the scene she'd witnessed in Natalie's kitchen that night. She'd written it off as an impulsive moment, a sorry-I-got-carried-away-it-won't-happen-again accident. Blair's cynicism about relationships stopped at the border of Annie and Natalie's, even though she joked about their coupledom, their inseparability. Ham and eggs, milk and cookies, Annie and Natalie — she'd make comparisons to tease them. Bread and butter. Why had she believed in them and not others? She hadn't been drawn in by Natalie's long speeches on the joys of wedded bliss, or the need for their community to begin establishing its own traditions. What had hooked Blair was the example Natalie and Annie offered of a couple who had worked through their problems. Their way of being together, the atmosphere of ease and comfort that permeated their house, all their gatherings, spoke louder than a thousand promises and impromptu speeches at birthday parties.

At the table, the commitment question was still being turned inside out, examined from all sides. Blair rose.

"You can't leave now," Leah protested. "This is an important discussion."

"I am definitely not the person to be talking to about relationships." She crossed the room to help Natalie clear platters from the buffet table. She said, "You were unusually reticent tonight, counselor." That ought to leave Natalie a wide enough opening.

"Take my advice: when you get to thirty-nine, stay there."

Blair followed her into the kitchen. "And not have a swell party like this?"

"I'm too old for parties," Natalie griped playfully.

"I heard that," Tess said, whisking Natalie back to the table.

Blair was left wondering about Natalie. She knew something dark lurked beneath the playful banter. Blair had listened to too many tales of too many unhappy relationships; she recognized the signs. She was often the only unattached person at a party like tonight's. Not consumed by the needs of another, she was able to observe couples and the little games they played. Like Nicole and Emma. Tonight Emma didn't like Nicole's finishing her sentences for her. Emma hadn't said anything, merely made a point of saying, each time Nicole committed the offense, "No, that wasn't what I meant." Blair could write a book on the little slights and tiny arguments that presaged the first stage of trouble, minute differences in behavior. Like Natalie's unusual distraction, her uneasiness and reticence. Her uncharacteristic avoidance of the topic of relationships. Annie, on the other hand, was too voluble, pouring unnecessary words into every silence.

But then how long could you be a model couple? No reason Natalie and Annie should be immune from the problems other couples had. As a single woman, Blair was everyone's choice as confidante; no matter how happy a couple professed to be, it seemed there was always some drama going on. Why should she be so shocked when Natalie and Annie finally fell to Blair's law?

She congratulated herself for not being involved with anyone. She didn't understand everyone's need to be attached to another person, or their fear of being alone. Looking around the room, she realized she and Leah were the only single women at the party. And Leah was always, and desperately, trying to change that situation. Even Tess was crossing over into the ranks of coupledom with Sarah. Everyone, it seemed, wanted in. But did Natalie actually want out? Blair had trouble making sense of that one. She drained the last of her scotch, wondering if she should have another before she left. She glanced at her watch.

"Got a hot date?" Annie asked.

"As a matter of fact, I do." She was meeting Roxanne after the party.

"Ah, single people's time." Annie smiled. "As I crawl gratefully into bed at a decent hour, I think of you poor souls cruising around town, just getting to the latest bar as I drift blissfully to sleep."

Blair knew what Annie meant. Often her evenings didn't start until long after her married friends were in for the night. She thought nothing of going over to a new lover's house at eleven, or later. Like tonight, they got together after separate dinner parties, or a concert, or after the bars closed.

"Why didn't you bring her?" Annie asked.

Blair merely shrugged. "Maybe next time." The real reason was that she didn't want Roxanne to get the wrong impression about the seriousness of their relationship. Across the room, Natalie was being given a lesson in advanced yo-yo. "What did Natalie say about the tickets? Was she blown away?"

"I think she was pleased."

Blair had to stop herself from exclaiming, Pleased about a first class trip to Paris? *Pleased?*

She heard the fear in her friend's voice as Annie jumped in to fill the silence. "It's hard to tell what she thinks these days. She's really under the gun at work. We'll probably go when things have slowed down for her."

The torrent of words gushed from Annie, as if she hoped to be carried to safety on the current.

• • • • •

Blair arrived at the club before Roxanne. Sometimes she wondered why she often ended up sitting in these bars either with or waiting for someone. The places no longer held any charm for her. They were dark, smoky, crowded and noisy. She no longer needed the reinforcement she'd once gotten from being around so many other lesbians. And now the crowd was a bit young for her. She'd outgrown the dramas and the fights, the jealousies and intrigues acted out in the space of an extended re-mix of a song. Yet she couldn't see herself sitting quietly at home week after week.

She eyed the restless women circling the dance floor, the regulars easy to spot, always on the move, greeting friends, chatting with the bartender. A woman two seats away at the bar offered to buy her a drink. Blair declined. "I'm waiting for someone. But thanks." As if on cue, Roxanne arrived, slightly out of breath and smiling. "Sorry I'm late. Have you been waiting long?"

"No. What would you like?"

"Let's just dance."

Roxanne moved well, smooth and sexy, and Blair thought of their dancing as an enjoyable prelude to what would follow.

They stopped to cool off, not talking much, content to stand side by side watching women dance. They went back onto the floor when a slow song started, leaning into each other, Roxanne's arms sliding up around Blair's neck, Blair's hands resting in the small of Roxanne's back. This was the closest they'd been, their first embrace. Roxanne rested her head against Blair's shoulder as Blair gently guided them across the crowded floor. Before the song ended Roxanne nudged herself still closer, raised her head, mouth to Blair's ear so that Blair felt as well as heard her breath, and a shiver ran through her as Roxanne said, "Let's go back to my place."

"What a great apartment!" Blair exclaimed as soon as she stepped into a living room that could have been in New Mexico.

"I did a film in Santa Fe two years ago, can you tell?" Roxanne placed her keys on a beat-up library table near her front door. Everything was in bleached, muted colors, the hardwood floors covered by pale area rugs. Even the patches of clutter, like the messy pile of design magazines and knick-knacks on the coffee table, seemed carefully thought out, the general effect of the room simple and clean. A modern cut-glass vase held a bunch of dramatically lit tulips.

A warm breeze stirred the gauzy curtains as the women sat in the living room with their drinks. They talked for a while, soft music playing in the background, the sexual urgency they'd felt on the dance floor tempered somewhat by the ride to Roxanne's in separate cars.

In the very back of her mind, Blair felt an ever so slight tug of memory, the vaguest whisper of Hallie. But Roxanne's voice was soothing and she was touching Blair, running her hand along Blair's arm, down her thigh. Besides, she didn't really look much like Hallie at all. Blair leaned to kiss Roxanne, wondering why she hadn't thought to do this sooner, this one simple act that would obliterate the past and ground her totally in the present.

Their clothes strewn about the room, they lay on the couch covered with a Pendleton blanket. Blair felt warm and lazy after their intense and energetic sex.

Roxanne turned on her side to face Blair. "So tell me about this woman I remind you of."

"You're really not very much alike at all. And I knew her a long time ago." Another lifetime, it seemed now.

"What was she like?" Roxanne persisted.

"Why is it so important to you?"

"Curiosity. I guess I just want you to be going out with me, not with whoever I remind you of." Roxanne traced her finger around Blair's mouth, trailed it along her cheeks, down her neck across her shoulder, her arm.

Hallie's shadow had faded from Blair's mind until Roxanne brought up the subject. "Don't worry, you're not really like her at all. Come here." She put an arm around Roxanne, who nestled against her shoulder. Blair closed her eyes, trying to retreat to that warm, lazy place she'd been in only moments earlier.

Sometimes when reading in bed, just before she fell asleep she would hear a voice in her head, calling her name or saying something she couldn't quite understand. Lying next to Roxanne, half-dozing, she heard Hallie say her name. Startled, Blair opened her eyes. She hadn't heard that voice in nine years, and yet she knew it immediately. She sat up.

"What's the matter?" Roxanne asked sleepily.

"Go back to sleep." She stroked Roxanne's hair. "I've got to go home."

"I was hoping you'd stay . . ."

"Another time."

Roxanne tried to keep Blair from leaving, tempting her with offers of another drink, more sex, a warm bath, a back rub. But Blair's need to escape the sound of Hallie's voice — and this woman who reminded her so much of Hallie, no matter how she denied it — was urgent and compelling.

The drive home didn't clear her head of the pictures of Hallie. She tried recalling the events of the evening — Natalie's party, dancing with Roxanne, making love. She tried to break it down even further by visualizing the smallest details — her fumbling with the silver buckle on Roxanne's tooled leather belt, working Roxanne's soft cotton shirt down over her shoulders — but still her mind kept substituting Hallie for Roxanne. Each time she tried to recall Roxanne's face she saw Hallie's, so that it became Hallie, not Roxanne, whom she'd led around the dance floor, Hallie she'd made love to earlier, Hallie who had called her name over and over and over as she came.

Blair fought hard to stay away from a seductive and dangerous past. But so precise were her recollections that she could almost smell the dusting of cinnamon on the cappuccino they'd sipped late one afternoon in a tiny North Beach café.

They'd been at the hospital with her father since mid-morning without a break. The sun and the blue sky and the freedom of being out on the street were exhilarating, she was struck by the brilliance of everything she saw — gaudy neon advertising strip joints, a blue boat on a billboard, a student's bright red windbreaker. The hospital was a place drained of color. From the corridors to the bland prints on the walls in the patients' room, everything was beige or taupe. Flower arrangements from well-wishers — their once-loud reds and yellows the only splash of hue in her father's room — had wilted and grown brittle, their water brackish and foul, their odor lingering in a dark corner after the vases and baskets had been removed so that Blair had mistaken it for the smell of illness.

Even away from that room Blair carried with her the sounds of the hospital: discreet bells to call the nurse, phones ringing on the floor, doctors calling in orders for patients; the clatter of rolling metal carts laden with food trays or clean linen. She still heard the moans or groans or occasional laughter of patients and the artificially cheerful voices of visitors. The hospital had different sounds for day and night, its breathing more subdued after dark.

This bright day she sat with Hallie, Andrew had been in the hospital for four weeks. Blair's days were much the same, a routine of work/hospital/home with only slight variations. Hallie came with her sometimes, like today, and Andrew talked and joked with her, even flirted a little. He never lost that knack or desire.

For the last two weeks Andrew had trod a thin line between life and death, alternating between moments of lucidity and vision. He talked to his parents, long dead, whom he saw clearly in the room, standing opposite Blair and Hallie. He'd point them out to the women.

What astounded Blair almost as much as the process she was watching was the fact that for the first time in her life someone in her family was making contact with her.

Before, they had dealt with each other only at great distance. Even something as little as her father's laughing at a joke gave Blair an inordinate amount of pleasure. When she got her first job after art school she knew he was proud of her because she overheard him say so to her aunt. But no words had ever passed directly between them.

And now this stunning inclusion in his voyage — Blair had no time to discuss forgiveness or regrets with her father, she could only respond to events of the moment.

He told Blair about his parents, how they were waiting for him to join them.

"Is it nice where they are?" Blair softly asked.

Andrew smiled. "That's the place to be."

When her father shared that glimpse of his future with her, it was as if a door to an empty room inside her were opening. She had an image of herself on the threshold of that room, peering in with curiosity. It seemed to her, too, like a wonderful place to be.

An extraordinary peace visited them all that afternoon. A serenity that lasted until Constance came barging in, her mouth arranged in its best hospital volunteer smile, a high beam aimed to cheer up even the gloomiest patient. Blair and Hallie left soon after Constance's arrival.

"I don't know if I could get through this without you," Blair said to Hallie in the café that warm afternoon.

"You could get through it without me, but you

don't have to." Hallie took Blair's hand across the table.

Even after the long morning waiting for Andrew to die, Blair felt desire for Hallie, a hunger that surprised her. Looking at her, Blair saw a safe place. Hallie's beauty shone through the mood of the day. Not taking her eyes from Hallie's, Blair brought Hallie's hand to her lips, opened the palm and softly kissed it. Blair had never said "I love you" to anyone. But today the words were there, though unspoken, and Hallie knew this because Hallie said, "Me too."

"I'm bushed," Blair said when they arrived at Hallie's apartment. She flopped on the couch, one arm covering her face.

"Come," Hallie said, taking her hand and leading her into the bathroom. She helped Blair undress, and got into the shower with her, soaping her body. Hallie wrapped her in a towel, led her into the tiny bedroom. She drew back the covers. "Lie down," she gently commanded.

Blair stretched out on her stomach. Hallie straddled her hips. She poured some lotion into her hand and began to massage Blair's back.

With each stroke, memories held in Blair's muscles were released to her brain. She was blinded by a kaleidoscopic barrage of pictures that came in no logical sequence or context. An image, vivid and startling, would spring up when Hallie touched a particular area. Flashes of a rare Sunday trip to Golden Gate Park with her father — where were Paul and her mother? — had been lodged in her trapezius. Hidden inside each knotted muscle were glimpses of more recent scenes from the hospital: a doctor's tapered fingers nervously fiddling with a rubber band as he told them that Andrew's condition was rapidly deteriorating; a young patient in a nearby room partying with his friends, offering take-out pizza and soda to the nurses. Tucked under her left shoulder blade was the way her father smelled when he came home from the office, his aftershave faint under a stale layer of leather and tobacco. Her neck was a repository of lost moments: a scolding from her mother for not cleaning up her room after repeatedly being told to do so; riding with Paul in the back seat of their father's new convertible, so proud of her handsome parents in the front, wanting someone she knew to see how good they looked in this rare display of family togetherness.

As Hallie worked down Blair's legs to the soles of her feet more images appeared on the screen in Blair's mind. Hallie spent a long time on her arms and hands, pulling the tension out of Blair's fingers. And with it the faint odors of the stale flowers in Andrew's room, the clatter of the hospital carts.

After the initial bombardment, the recognizable images that her mind threw onto the screen became abstract — dark cartoon scribbles that wiggled frantically, angrily, before exploding into the next batch. The barrage gradually diminished and faded, leaving a pure white, blank screen. Finally all pictures had been erased by Hallie's fingers, and were replaced by an image of Hallie's hands on her, isolating those areas of her body Hallie was touching, fingers seen in a detailed close-up. At last Blair was aware of nothing else. When she heard Hallie's voice, it came from far away. "Okay, flip over."

144

Blair obeyed, resting her hands on Hallie's thighs. Hallie began to smooth lotion on Blair's chest. Blair took some herself, rubbing her palms together before moving them up Hallie's hips and back. She slid them under Hallie's arms, around to her chest, pausing to feel the weight of Hallie's breasts as she leaned over Blair. Hallie's massaging rhythm became erratic as Blair's became more sure. Blair sat up, Hallie still straddling her, and they held each other a long while before they kissed.

Blair's lips moved from Hallie's mouth to her throat, her shoulders, her breasts. Hallie leaned back now, arms behind her for support, head thrown back, eyes closed. Her hips circled slowly as Blair slid herself down so she was between Hallie's thighs.

The light of the moon entered the tiny bedroom that night as Hallie and Blair thrashed on the bed and the covers slipped to the floor. Blair knelt on the rug by the side of the bed. Soon they were both on the floor, Blair reaching for a pillow to slide under Hallie's hips. As the women struggled together the startlingly huge yellow-orange globe that had risen earlier transformed itself into the boring perfection of a full moon.

Close to coming, Blair again saw herself on the threshold of that room inside herself, saw Hallie beckoning to her from within. The room looked warm and inviting.

"Say what you were going to say this afternoon," Hallie whispered.

"You know."

"But say the words. Because of the moon — tell me you love me."

Blair lay on her back, Hallie between her legs. The beauty of the moment too dangerous for her.

Hallie pulled away from her, panting from her exertions. "Help me, Blair, please."

But something was in the air that night, in the light of the moon, and whatever it was kept Blair from giving herself to Hallie, and from setting foot in that room.

Blair arrived at the hospital only minutes after her father died. Flo, the nurse he liked so much, told Blair he'd gone peacefully.

Blair was aware for the first time of a small, dark hole in the center of her being. Small, but seeming of infinite depth. The tears she'd been restraining came then, and Flo held her. She cried for herself as much as for her father.

Only much later did she go to Hallie's apartment. "Why didn't you call me," Hallie said, stroking Blair's hair. "I would have come right over."

Blair couldn't tell her that it was easier to be held by a stranger.

All these years Blair thought she had pinpointed the exact moment she'd first recognized that cold, hollow spot, dating it from the time she'd learned about Andrew's death. It had bled like an ink drop on white cloth, spreading only so far before setting indelibly inside her as she cried. Only now did the thought occur to her that maybe it had lain there

146

undetected since that bright day when she kissed Hallie's hand and looked into her eyes in the café and couldn't speak the words she felt.

Driving away from Roxanne's, Blair struggled with her memories. She knew only too well where they were headed. Try as she would, she was unable to divert them as they led her to their inevitable conclusion.

When she escaped San Francisco, she said she was leaving Hallie behind because Hallie, like Constance, demanded too much of her.

Now, so many years later, Blair knew she'd done it because she'd seen Hallie, not as her too needy lover, but as one more person to be taken from her, one more potential for loss.

When Blair arrived home she went right to the liquor cabinet and poured herself a cognac, the most effective palliative for the ice cold hollow core inside her. Downing it in one gulp, she quickly poured another and finished off that one, too, before making her way to bed.

Chapter Eight
Out of the Frying Pan

Natalie was very restless and ill at ease. She dated the onset of her condition — one her uncle Souran called Nervous and Jerky — from right after Maggie left the office for another job. She was unable to sit still, to remain seated, to be calm. Hearing a deposition, her foot fluttered on its own, sometimes setting her whole leg jiggling as if it wanted to run off somewhere. To counter that flight she'd been forced more than once to throw her arm out for balance — over the back of a chair, onto the table — in hopes of steadying her suddenly recalcitrant body.

The Monday after her birthday a few of the attorneys in the firm organized a little party for her. They all gathered in the conference room, opened a bottle of sparkling cider, and toasted her arrival into middle age. Natalie accepted their wishes for many happy returns, along with a package from Nieman-Marcus — a black leather briefcase with her initials blind embossed on the front.

"It's gorgeous," she exclaimed, modeling it against her side.

Though her secretary had ordered a cake for the occasion, luckily no one asked Natalie to make a speech, and the party broke up soon after the cake was served. Back in her office, Natalie sat with her new bag on her lap, her palms on the smooth leather. She inhaled its rich scent, traced her fingers over the indentation made by her initials. NJB. This was a formidable case. What had Jack Korbin said about it, that it befit her station?

But what exactly was her station? Who did people think she was?

A few weeks earlier, she'd been in a bookstore on a Saturday afternoon and heard someone call her name. She turned to see Cassandra Ryder, her associate, approaching. "I almost didn't recognize you without a suit on," Cassandra had said.

Lately it seemed to her that only Maggie had seen beyond that person in the suit. With the exception of joke presents, little toys and games, she'd been given an unexciting array of gifts for her birthday. Not that she was ungrateful or unappreciative, but the presents confirmed her worst fears about her image:

everyone saw her as a no-nonsense, down to earth, practical person. She herself barely remembered her old reputation as a playful troublemaker. Ever since grade school her friends had looked to her to shake up their routine with an adventure, and she always accommodated them. Uncles and aunts and cousins could each tell at least one story starting with, "I remember the time Natalie . . ." As late as college she still had the power to surprise, though it had taken Laura's stories at lunch to remind Natalie of that. Now she left it to Annie to be the unpredictable one, the adventurer. Natalie had settled into some other role.

When she first started in practice, she hadn't been out of pants for eight years. After years in sweaters and jeans she had put on suits, silk blouses, and heels. Now the image she presented matched everyone's visual perception of what a woman attorney should look like.

Originally, it had been necessary for her to pose as that super-self-confident woman. The woman in the suit had been an impostor masquerading as Natalie Bazarian, the impostor's toughness serving Natalie well in her dealings with developers and politicians and other attorneys. But now the impostor was impossible to shake, and she chafed at the demands it made upon her.

Mostly it wanted her to maintain her edge, that competitive streak that would protect her from the Parker Shermans of the world. But Natalie wasn't so sure that was what she wanted anymore.

Just as she was no longer willing or able to be the standard bearer for her community. She'd felt like a hypocrite on her birthday, when everyone talked about her and Annie as their "family." She'd been on display that night as one half of the model couple that was Annie and Natalie. The memory of her birthday brought on a foot-tapping that demanded distraction.

She fished Maggie's present out of her desk drawer. She held up an earring, watching its surface catch the light. Not even the prospect of a trip to Paris excited her the way the hammered silver and gold leaf did. The earrings were here before her. Paris was far away, in a future she could no longer visualize. She was just starting to try the earrings on when the phone rang.

At first the interruption of the call from Jeremy was a relief. Immersion in work was the only thing that kept her from thinking. But the relief was only temporary.

"Did Parker go over the new plans with you?" Jeremy asked.

"What new plans?"

"He ran some ideas by me over dinner last night —"

Oh great, Natalie thought. Now they're having dinner together. Jeremy probably thought of Parker as the son he never had.

Jeremy was talking through his speaker phone, and his voice came to her from a great distance. Jeremy rarely did just one thing at a time. She could hear him shuffling papers, his voice receding as he walked around the room. His intercom buzzed, and she heard his secretary announce a call from a state senator.

"Sorry, Natalie, this is about a variance I've been trying to get. Have Parker fill you in on his ideas on the drive down tomorrow."

"I wasn't planning on bringing him with me."

"Well, maybe you should. It'll be good exposure for him. He's rough around the edges, but he's got a lot of initiative, and I want him to learn from you."

Natalie felt sick. The meeting at Bridge Creek was routine. The utility company had an easement for part of the land Jeremy was trying to develop, and the engineer dealing with the issue realized he needed Natalie's help. She had set up the conference with six representatives of the utility company to talk about removing or re-locating the easement. And she knew that Parker was no threat to her — yet. No matter how good his ideas were, he would need her expertise to execute them. But he had set her up again, and she didn't like that. And she didn't like that he was getting so chummy with Jeremy.

She called Annie. "I might be home late. I've got to prepare for this meeting in Riverside."

"I thought it was just routine." Annie was in the middle of an edit and her distraction translated on Natalie's end of the line into the click of buttons on the editing console, blips of music as she cued to the exact frame she wanted.

"It is, but I still need to prepare for it," Natalie said.

"Whatever," Annie mumbled. "What about dinner?"

"I just told you, I'll be late."

"Right. Sorry, but I'm trying to make this deadline."

Natalie heard more clicks, garbled dialogue. Someone in the editing room was talking to Annie.

Annie came back on the line. "If you won't be home, I'll probably stay late and try to get this done — it might take all night."

Natalie heard the squeak of voices on fast forward, rustling of papers — probably Annie's cue sheet. "Annie . . ."

"What, honey?" Annie asked impatiently.

Clearly this wasn't the time to talk to Annie about Parker Sherman. "Nothing. I'll talk to you later."

"If you call, try me here first."

"Okay."

As Natalie hung up a huge wave of emptiness swept over her. She felt completely separated from herself. She looked out the window. Her mood darkened in direct contrast to the sunlit exterior. She buzzed her secretary. "I'll be gone for the rest of the day, Sandra. Tell Parker I'll meet him at the site tomorrow morning."

She drove without knowing where she was going until she suddenly exited the freeway and steered through a peaceful residential neighborhood. Parked on a quiet street, she sat in the car, drumming a staccato beat on the steering wheel. Natalie had looked up Maggie's address weeks ago.

An easy good feeling hung over the street. Birds sang. The intrusive whir of a leaf blower started up a few houses away. She sat in the car until the buzzing stopped and the clear birdsongs came through again. A dog barked somewhere; she heard the rustle and scrape of leaves being raked off concrete. She had the same feeling as when she was a child and sick enough to stay home from school but not too sick to enjoy it: the delight at being in the house and neighborhood at times she wasn't usually around, dozing in quiet rooms flooded with sunlight, her mother pampering her with hot chocolate. Fighting back a fierce nostalgia for the simplicity of those days, she locked her car and walked up a flower-lined path.

She knew Maggie had class Monday night and often spent the afternoon in the library preparing for it, so there was a good chance no one would be home. Or maybe Maggie would be here with someone else. Natalie checked the mailboxes, found Maggie's name. She walked through the courtyard. Maggie's apartment was on the second floor in back. God, this was a dumb idea. She felt like a teenager, not a forty-year-old. Her heart was pounding, her pulse beat in her ears. But not from panic. This was different. She rang the bell, waited. Maggie probably wasn't here. Just as well. She'd leave a note. Natalie braced her foot against the door jamb, balancing her briefcase on her knee. She was fumbling for her pen when the door opened, and she practically fell into Maggie's apartment.

Practically fell into Maggie, hair wrapped in a towel, wearing a terry robe and smelling of soap and green leaves, a damp, sweet smell.

"I wasn't sure I heard the bell. Come on in." Maggie wrapped her robe more tightly around herself. "I'll just put something on." She hurried back down the hall.

Natalie stepped inside, closing the door behind her.

The apartment was small, if she could judge from this main room, which was living room, dining room, and foyer in one. She could see into the tiny kitchen from where she stood. A short hall led to a bathroom and the bedroom off to the right.

Maggie had the basics in furniture: couch, coffee table, one armchair. What in a normal apartment would have been the dining room table had been converted into Maggie's desk. Natalie recognized the signs of a law student: the good lamp, *Black's Law Dictionary* next to *The Attorney's Pocket Dictionary*, marking pens in every color, stacks of notes and textbooks and outlines. In addition to a few prints on the wall, Maggie had tacked up menus from neighborhood take-out restaurants. Except for the clutter of books and papers, the place was very neat.

Natalie stood in the middle of the room, thinking this was crazy, wondering why she'd come, whether or not she should leave. She had a flash of home — Annie carrying her birthday cake, that proud smile on her face. She pushed the image from her mind. She was in the center of this small apartment, this uncluttered life. A carefully structured haven. Maybe things really could be this simple. No time to think about it, though, because Maggie was walking towards her from the bedroom, smiling and saying, "Don't you want to put your briefcase down?"

Maggie had returned wearing pale yellow sweatpants and a navy T-shirt. How could anyone look sexy like that? But she did. Her hair was still damp. She still smelled green and sweet. Sunlight flooded the room, overexposing the tan couch and rug. Maggie pointed to the couch. "Would you like to sit down?"

"I can't stay." *What am I doing here?*

"Is that a new briefcase?" Maggie asked, breaking the awkward silence.

Natalie looked down. She'd forgotten she had anything in her hand. "A birthday present from everyone."

"It's beautiful."

Natalie looked at it, glad to have something to talk about. "I know. I like it even though Parker picked it out. He might be an opportunist, but he's got good taste, our bright new star."

"He's not that bright," Maggie said. "He kept coming on to me. Wouldn't take no for an answer. I think he thought I left the firm to get away from him."

Natalie couldn't help smiling at that. Their shared moment of delight at Parker's expense loosened Natalie up enough to say, "Thank you for the earrings."

"You're welcome. They're collector's items now. Sydney's off to some ashram in New England. Who knows if she'll ever be heard from again."

Natalie wanted to respond with something witty, but she couldn't speak. She couldn't move. She put her briefcase on the floor near her feet, but that was all she could manage. Her peripheral vision clouded, she saw nothing but Maggie standing four feet away from her. While her mind was discoursing on commitment, her body began moving towards Maggie, fully resolved. Just like that afternoon in her office.

Coming here was a mistake. *Say good-bye and then get out.* Resolved to do just that, she opened her mouth, heard her own voice saying, "You're so very beautiful."

Maggie stepped forward, close enough now to touch. "Are you sure this time?"

Natalie put her hand out, drew Maggie towards her.

It was so easy. All that tortuous time of thinking and reasoning and denying — who cared about Parker Sherman or the impostor or anything else? Here was Maggie. As Natalie stared into those cat eyes, her hands moved under Maggie's shirt, rested lightly on her back. That smooth skin! "Wait," Maggie said. In one motion she stepped back and drew her shirt over her head. Natalie reached for her again. The easiest thing in the world. She maintained her balance by leaning into their kiss.

They never made it to the bedroom. Not even to the couch. They sank to the floor where they were. Natalie reached greedily for Maggie, as if angry for the time she'd wasted before, time they had been denied. Maggie pulled Natalie's shirt out of her skirt, tugged impatiently at the silk tie. Together they worked at the buttons with trembling fingers, peeled down the pantyhose. At last. In the flood of sensations Natalie could only hold on to certain details. The itchy carpet was noted and instantly forgotten. But Maggie's warm soft skin and the fresh green scent of leaves filled her head. So close now to Maggie, Natalie saw everything in chiaroscuro patterns — the navy T-shirt bunched under Maggie's shoulder, bright patches of skin, the base of the couch, Maggie's eyes, her own dark suit in a heap. She was aware, too, of the briefcase nearby, with its new leather smell. But then all was Maggie. The hot sun shone in on them, intensifying everything. The light seemed to magnify the fine hairs on Maggie's skin, highlighted the thin film of moisture in the small of her back. The light did not dim when Natalie finally closed her eyes, unable to take in any more.

In moving from the living room floor to the bedroom Natalie stumbled over her briefcase. Poor Parker, she thought, following Maggie down the corridor.

Making love with Maggie was timeless. Natalie had no idea how long she'd been in the apartment. For once, it didn't matter. Suddenly all her motions and gestures could be channelled into something. All that energy now directed towards one goal.

Most astonishing to her was that even in the midst of their urgent haste, their rush to discover each other, she was moving towards calm. So intent had she been on pleasing Maggie that awareness of her own state of mind surprised her. Her uncontrolled shakings and twitches had become circles. Everything round: the motion of Maggie's fingers on her, the answering rhythm of her hips; her legs raised now, circled behind Maggie's back. And now circles of feeling as she came, waves radiating out from Maggie's hand on her, in her, circles through her body. And out her mouth, circles again, as she cried out, a loud, extended round "Ohhh," before collapsing, silent again, and finally, blissfully, perfectly — still.

When Natalie woke, it was dark. Maggie was still sleeping. Natalie made her way into the living room. She had to call Annie. The enormity of what she'd done hadn't sunk in yet. Annie was somewhere deep inside her, in a place she couldn't go near. Not yet. She didn't know how she was going to tell this lie.

No one answered at work. Annie was probably still cutting. Natalie tried the house, was grateful to get the machine. She left a message that she would be working through the night, would shower at the office and leave for Riverside by six the next morning. Nothing unusual about that. Except the lie.

She stepped into Maggie's shower. She stood for a long time under the spray, adjusting the head to massage, then back to regular. Not that she needed to feel any more relaxed than she already did. It had been so long since she'd experienced that totally spent feeling after hours of lovemaking. She ached in a wonderful way, and a sweet heavy lethargy sat in her body.

She reached for the shampoo, a kind she'd never

seen before. She enjoyed the new smells and sounds around her: the hollow shuddering through the pipes when she turned up the hot water; the green apple bath soap; the shampoo, a dark brown, unappetizing liquid. She opened the bottle and took a whiff of the murky stuff. It smelled like crushed green leaves, not herbal, just green. Much stronger than the scent in Maggie's hair. Woods in the rain.

The glass door slid open and Maggie stepped into the shower. Maggie lathered her hands, then soaped Natalie's body. Natalie turned them both around, changing positions so Maggie would be under the spray. "Don't want you to get cold."

Natalie poured more shampoo onto her hand, began lathering Maggie's hair. "What is this stuff, anyway?"

"It's made with walnut leaves. Takes a little getting used to."

Natalie wondered if she would get used to any of this.

They stepped out of the shower, hurriedly wrapping each other in towels, rubbing briskly to stave off the chill. Their quick movements gave way to slower ones, and soon they were back in bed.

Weak grey light outlined the drawn window shades, but the room was still dark. Natalie couldn't remember at first where she was. When she saw Maggie sleeping next to her, waves of grief and guilt overpowered the excitement she'd felt the night before. Everything she'd been able to hold at bay came flooding through her, memories and feelings tumbling pell-mell over each other in a rush to torment her, the vows she and Annie had exchanged at their commitment ceremony echoing hollowly in her head. She couldn't reconcile the double images: the flesh and blood person padding barefoot around Maggie's dark bedroom, the mental image of herself as Annie's faithful mate and partner for life.

Maggie's alarm clock chirped, and Maggie's arm moved lazily to stifle the sound. Despite the guilt and shame, Natalie couldn't look at the sleeping figure without wanting to crawl in bed next to her and take up where they'd left off. But that wasn't an option. She'd have to shower and dress quickly in order to make it to Riverside in time for her meeting. She stumbled towards the bathroom in the dark. *What have I done? How could I do this to Annie?*

And then she was bounced towards that forbidden area. Because she wanted to be with Maggie. Needed the joy and passion of the night she'd just spent.

Instead of being exhausted, Natalie felt invigorated.

Hours of sex and talk. And laughter. Just like she'd heard from Leah and Hildy through the walls in Palm Springs. Wild and daring sex, performed with an abandon she'd imagined was gone from her life. "Not bad for forty," she'd crowed at one point. Stretched out next to each other, panting and sweating from their exertions, Natalie said "I feel like I've got this idiotic grin on my face, but I can't get rid of it."

Maggie turned to look at her. "It looks good on you. You should wear it more often."

161

Natalie faced Maggie, took her hand. "I'm not sure how often that's going to be." She kissed Maggie's hand.

"Hey, don't get serious on me now," Maggie said. "I know you're married. Being with you tonight is great. I don't expect anything." Maggie slid herself on top of Natalie, silencing her thoughts as well as her words.

A doubting, guilty woman had stepped naked into the bathroom. Out of it emerged the impostor, impeccably groomed, authoritative. She left Maggie a brief note and was in her car and on the freeway within half an hour from the time she'd first opened her eyes.

Stuck in bumper-to-bumper traffic, she focused on the day ahead of her. No one would be in the office yet, but she made notes of what she needed to tell Sandra. Shifting into business mode would be the best way to forget about what she'd done, at least for a while. But every time she remembered she was forgetting, she felt a little tingle between her legs, in her stomach. How could she want Maggie so much and at the same time feel so guilty about it? Surely the guilt should cancel out the desire.

Out of a sense of duty or force of habit she reached for the car phone and tried the house. Luckily, the machine picked up, because she had no idea what to say to Annie. She left a message that she'd be in touch later that afternoon. She didn't try the office; that would have been pushing her luck.

Although she had resolved not to talk to Maggie until she had seen Annie, Natalie called her next. "Good morning."

"What a nice surprise," Maggie said, her voice thick with sleep.

"Did I wake you?"

"Someone kept me up all night. Where are you?"

"On the Santa Monica Freeway." Natalie inched the car along as she talked. She wanted to say, Let's get together again. Thoughts like, Last night really meant a lot to me, or, I think I could fall in love with you, kept coming to her. She wanted to have the kind of sexy morning-after conversation their night before merited. But her guilt made her almost cool to Maggie. "I don't know what to do about Annie," she ended up saying, not having planned to get into this at all.

"You don't have to do anything about her."

Natalie said sharply, "Meaning what, that I've already done enough?"

"Meaning you don't have to tell her."

That option had certainly occurred to Natalie.

"Look, whatever you decide," Maggie said, "last night was wonderful. That won't change."

No, thought Natalie, but everything else has.

Parker Sherman was waiting for her at the Bridge Creek site. After a few minutes, the representative of the utility company showed up, and the three of them drove to the area of the easement.

The ache in Natalie's legs as she walked the uneven terrain to the exact location of the easement reminded her of the positions she'd been in the night before. She kept floating off from the details in front of her, and was glad Parker was there to keep track of the proceedings. She could still smell Maggie, hear the sounds they'd made.

When they were finished at the site, having come to enough of an agreement to set up another meeting at her office to begin to draw up papers, Natalie suggested that she and Parker stop for coffee before driving back to L.A. This would put them on the freeway during the height of rush hour traffic, but she would do anything to postpone the inevitable meeting with Annie.

Too preoccupied now with the dread of facing Annie, with figuring out what she would do, Natalie let Parker do the talking. Maggie could wait. Natalie's responsibility was to Annie. But what about her responsibility to herself? For once in her life, couldn't she do what she wanted to do? That resolve encouraged her. Oblivious to Parker, she cut him off mid-sentence, saying she had to get going. She reached for the check. He offered to pay, but she said "It'll be your treat when you make partner."

Chapter Nine
Balancing Acts

As Lillian Webb had predicted, Blair had gotten the Dinnertime account. And, as Blair had predicted, it was proving to be a difficult assignment, not because of the work involved, but because of the client. Lillian was relentless in her pursuit. What had started as a harmless flirtation was becoming a very sticky problem.

Blair enjoyed flirting, she had no objection to the innuendo and double entendres scattered throughout

Lillian's conversation. She was adept at staying out of harm's way if she chose. But when Lillian progressed from words to chance touches — hands, knees, shoulders, any part of Blair's body that could be grazed accidentally — Blair withdrew into the work in front of her. She kept her head down and her eyes on her drawing board.

Lillian was demanding; she sought out Blair's presence. Business that could have been dealt with over the phone had to be conducted face to face. At one such unnecessary meeting Lillian interrupted Blair.

"Wait, you're losing me."

"Okay." Blair patiently stopped. She had been explaining her choice of a background color. "The blue I used before blended too much with —"

"That's not where I got lost." Lillian traced her fingers along Blair's lips. "This is where I had trouble." And then she leaned forward and kissed where her fingers had traced.

Blair did not return the kiss.

"Don't say anything," Lillian softly commanded.

Blair did nothing except sit very still.

Lillian continued. "I'm going to make you an offer. Nothing has to happen between us, but I'd like it if something did. I'd like it very much. You may not think so, but I can be quite patient, and I'm willing to wait for what I want."

With her proposition on the table, Lillian was ready to resume work. She made no further reference to what had passed between them, and her casual touches and meaningful glances ceased. She asked only valid questions about the layout, and listened to Blair's answers. She trusted Blair's judgement implicitly. In that respect, Lillian Webb was an ideal client.

Blair went back to her office in a cloud of confusion that clung to her for the rest of the day. She was unaccustomed to being in this position.

Even if she wasn't always the initiator, she always maintained control, she played the game on her terms. Her subtle and harmless flirtations at work had no serious intent behind them. She could flirt with men because she knew it would never go past that stage. She took more care with women. She was, after all, very professional, and wouldn't do anything at this point to jeopardize her career. She'd never had to deal with anyone like Lillian Webb before. Not at work, anyway.

Blair sat hunched over her board finishing up the schematics — miniatures of the different flavors of the Down Home meals — when Lillian called to say she wanted to stop by the office to take a look at the new spacing Blair had done on the logo.

"I'll be out, Lillian." Blair was grateful for the legitimate excuse. She had promised to take Ted, her neighbor, to his doctor's appointment. "I'll fax you a pencil drawing of it."

"We can meet later," Lillian offered. "I'll be here until at least six-thirty or seven."

"I won't be back in the office today," Blair said firmly.

Lillian Webb was not one to take no for an answer. "I wanted to take a look at the new colors, too. How about tomorrow morning? We could have breakfast."

"I'll just messenger everything to you, that'll be a lot simpler."

"But not nearly as pleasant."

Blair didn't have the stamina for Lillian's games today, but she reminded herself that it was her job to keep the client happy — even if Lillian was increasingly harder to dodge diplomatically. She put the schematics and the sketch of the new logo in a packet with a note: "How about a rain check on breakfast?" She dropped the package at the reception desk on her way out, telling Dana to be sure it got to the Dinnertime offices by three.

High, hot Santa Ana winds had swept the L.A. basin clear of smog, and Blair drove towards the beach rejoicing in the great weather. She felt like a kid out of school on a legitimate excuse. The afternoon was fine and full of possibilities. She could go for a run later or, if it stayed warm enough, sit out on the terrace and work.

Ted had said he'd leave the front door open for her, but Blair entered cautiously. Duncan, Ted's ex-lover and best friend, had told her about some of the episodes Ted had suffered — seizures and vomiting and diarrhea. Blair didn't think she could deal with any of that. What if something happened while she was with Ted? She hated herself for being afraid, but she was.

She called Ted's name as she walked into his living room. "I'm almost ready," he yelled down from the bedroom. Blair crossed to the window.

Ted's layout was the same as hers, but their tastes were totally opposite. She emphasized light or natural shades in her choice of furniture and rugs, while Ted selected textured wools and dark leather; he'd gone for a clubby look, one that suited him perfectly.

In his early forties, Ted had been very active both socially and politically. He'd cut back on his schedule shortly after his AIDS diagnosis, and had devoted himself to positive thinking and action. He'd changed his diet and his work habits, and had battled the disease for six years.

Today the afternoon sun drenched Ted's living room. Blair stood near the door to the terrace and looked out at a view almost identical to hers. A stunt kite spiraled and danced above the beach. A man walked the sand, eyes down, with a metal detector hovering above the surface like a divining rod; behind him he dragged a plastic garbage bag. Two young mothers pushed strollers past a trio of old ladies seated on a bench. A skate boarder skidded to a stop and flipped his board on its side, balancing on its edge a moment before flipping it back and skating through the whole routine again. A sad drunk poet in a wheelchair expounded unintelligibly to anyone who would listen. But no amount of activity could detract from the peace of the water and the sharp blue sky. A hot soft breeze fanned the perfect afternoon. Blair stood mesmerized by the sense of tranquility.

After perhaps ten minutes with no sign of Ted, she began to worry. She went to the foot of the stairs and called to him. "Ted? You okay?"

"Come on up."

Blair climbed the stairs. Ted sat on his bed. He had on his shirt, underwear, and socks. His pants lay next to him. "I've managed to get this far," he said, trying to sound chipper.

"Need some help?" Blair offered.

"I think so."

She crossed to the bed and knelt before him. She

took his pants and helped him put in first one foot, then the other.

Two years ago when they ran together, Blair had envied Ted's long, muscular legs. Now they were pale and thin. Only with great effort could he lift them so Blair could put his shoes on his feet. He used a cane to pull himself up off the bed.

Finally dressed, he moved so slowly it was obvious that even the slightest action pained him. Blair offered her arm as he inched towards the stairs, but Ted wouldn't take it. Instead, he balanced carefully on each step, a few times putting his arm out to the wall for support. It took ten minutes to get down the short flight, another ten to get from the apartment to the car.

Blair thumbed mindlessly through magazines while he was in with the doctor. She raged against this disease. She had witnessed Ted's transformation from go-getter to invalid. She couldn't imagine being in his position. They were almost the same age, after all, led similar lives, and should have been concerned about the same things. At this stage Blair hadn't begun to plan for her future, but at least she believed she had one.

In the car on the way home, she offered to stop at the market for him, but Ted said that Duncan was coming over with groceries and to fix dinner. When he was settled as comfortably as possible on his couch, Blair offered to make him tea, but he didn't want anything, and protested when Blair cleared away his lunch tray. "Duncan will do that when he gets here." Blair went ahead anyway. By the time she'd washed the dishes and was ready to leave, Ted was dozing.

Outside the hot winds had died down a little, but the air was still unseasonably warm. Blair tried unsuccessfully to work on some sketches, but ended up pouring herself a stiff drink and taking it out onto her balcony. She sat in the false summer until the light was nearly gone.

The sad drunk in the wheelchair was still parked near the sand. Blair longed for the distractions of the weekend crowd and the street performers. One of her favorites was a juggler with a great comedy routine. For the finale of each set, he would juggle three disparate items: a rubber chicken, a head of lettuce, and an M&M. The show ended when he caught the M&M in his mouth.

A vague restlessness sat over her, an unfocused anger. She briefly considered calling Lillian Webb — whether to encourage or discourage her she wasn't sure — but knew that either choice would lead to trouble. When Roxanne called and suggested dinner, Blair wondered sarcastically if this woman was her guardian angel. This was the second time Roxanne had saved her from herself.

Natalie's house looked the same. Outwardly, nothing had changed. She herself looked the same. She knew, because she'd checked in mirrors all day for visible evidence of her enormous interior transformation. She felt completely different, that same indescribable difference between being a virgin and not.

"You're home early," Annie said as she came up and kissed her. Natalie stiffened, imperceptibly, she hoped. Would Annie smell Maggie on her?

Apparently not. "I never left the office last night," Annie said. "We didn't finish until ten-thirty this morning. I came home and crashed. I don't know whether to have breakfast or dinner."

Annie didn't seem to suspect anything. "How about a drink first?" Natalie asked, trying to sound casual. So far, so good, but she really needed the drink.

Annie set out cheese and crackers while Natalie poured white wine for Annie and scotch for herself. "Did it go well?" Natalie asked as they moved around the kitchen.

Annie talked excitedly about the project. "It's exactly the kind of work I've wanted to do. Mark is a really creative director, but he needs me to organize him. He's got the ideas, but I know how to execute them."

"I haven't seen you this enthusiastic about something in a long time," Natalie said, getting up to refill her drink. Not that she'd heard much of what Annie had said. Better pay attention, she warned herself, though she knew she wasn't expected to understand too much technical talk.

"So let me tell you what I've been thinking about," Annie said. "Mark and I work really well together, and he's got more projects lined up. I've been toying with the idea in the back of my mind for a while, but then Mark mentioned something about it and, well, this could be a whole new direction." Annie paused, took a deep breath. "What would you think if I sold the business and went free lance?"

Natalie was too dumbfounded to say anything. Annie continued, "We can work out all the details, like whether I should actually sell the business or just my share and be a silent partner or something. But if I dumped the whole thing, I was thinking it would buy both of us some time off. We could travel. Use the Paris tickets."

During particularly busy periods they used to fantasize about taking off for six months or a year and driving around the country or going abroad. Annie was presenting the plan as a gift to her, Natalie could see that, but tonight this was dangerous ground, and her defenses were up. "Why didn't you tell me sooner?" Natalie asked.

"Mark only brought it up today."

"But you said you'd been thinking about it for a while."

"Well, I have." Annie paused for a long time.

"You're making major changes and not telling me?" Keep her on the defensive, thought Natalie.

"You've been preoccupied lately."

"So you're off planning your life without telling me about it?"

"Hey, I tried talking to you, Natalie. You haven't been around much to listen."

"Oh, so what should I do? Quit *my* job so we can both stay home and talk to each other?"

"This is getting out of hand," Annie said. "I know something's up."

Natalie jumped to attention.

"Why don't you tell me what's going on? I'm on your side, honey."

Annie's patience only made Natalie more impatient. "Why does something have to be going on? I've got more work than ever. The fair-haired boy of the firm is salivating for my job, and now he's got Jeremy Ives on his side —"

"You didn't tell me any of this," Annie interjected.

"I'm telling you now. Besides, it's no big deal. It's just a big hassle. But nothing's wrong, so lay off." Natalie's mind raced ahead. Her guilt was welling inside her, and she fought to contain it. "And as for being distant, I've got worked piled up to here —"

"Hey, calm down, I'm not saying it's intentional. I miss you, that's all. I miss little things, like throwing together a dinner like this." Annie leaned over and stroked Natalie's hair.

Natalie pulled away, knowing she couldn't sit across from Annie and maintain her self-righteous stance. She stood up. "I'm getting another drink. Want one?"

Annie shook her head no.

This wasn't turning out remotely the way Natalie had planned it. How naive she'd been to think she could keep up a front at home. It was hopeless to pursue this course. She'd have to tell Annie something.

Annie came into the kitchen with the dirty dishes. "What about Thanksgiving?"

"What about it?" Aside from its being the farthest thing from my mind, Natalie thought.

"Have you ordered the turkey?"

Thanksgiving at their house had become a tradition. Natalie shouldn't have felt like Annie was

174

pressuring her by asking what would have been, under normal circumstances, a logical question. But how could she pretend that in a little over a week she'd be merrily celebrating with their closest friends?

Annie was rattling on about what else they needed, reminding Natalie to round up their coffee urn from whomever had borrowed it last, telling her they'd have to start telling people what time to come.

What small remnant was left of Natalie's calm deserted her. Surely this was what it felt like to be drowning, the pressure getting stronger and squeezing the air out of your lungs, blood pumping so furiously you can no longer hear the churning water. All her instincts for survival raged so fiercely against the external force that Natalie could no longer hear the responses she was giving Annie. Annie had jumped back to Thanksgiving and was talking about place cards and how many cases of wine to buy while Natalie was caught in a whirlpool, forced underwater, unable to breathe. The pressure on her lungs was unbearable. "I was with someone last night," she blurted out.

"You what?" Annie said.

Too late now to call the words back. The pressure she'd released was between them, holding them separate from each other.

Annie sat perfectly still, looking at her. "This is a joke, right?"

The unnatural silence hung over them. Even the air around them was different.

Annie said, "I don't believe you."

The edges of the room fell away. She and Annie were floating in space.

Annie demanded: "Who?"

"It doesn't matter." Something inside Natalie had snapped, and she'd let go. She had found a still, dark place inside the turmoil where she could curl up and watch herself be sucked under the roiling current.

"Don't give me that crap," Annie said. "Who was it? Maggie?"

"That's not the issue."

"The fuck it isn't."

Natalie made no response.

"Come on," Annie urged her, "what's the issue here, then? You don't love me anymore?"

"I still love you," Natalie said quietly.

"You don't think I love you?"

No answer, until prodded, and then another, quieter, "That's not it."

"So what then?" Annie pressed on. "Is our life so bad? Maybe I've been missing something."

"No, it's my fault."

"Great. That's a start. Now that guilt had been established we're supposed to just go on from here —" Annie stopped abruptly. "Or are you planning to leave me?" She did not sound like she was pleading with Natalie to stay.

"I need some time to myself."

"You need *time*," Annie emphasized the word, "to fuck your brains out with this kid."

"She's not a kid."

"So it is Maggie." Annie seemed somewhat taken aback. "At least that's out in the open." She shook her head in disbelief. "I'm such a jerk." She looked at Natalie. "How could you do this?"

"I tried not to . . ."

"Is that supposed to make me feel better?" Annie

glared at her. "Maggie won't change what you're going through."

"You don't know what I'm going through," Natalie said defiantly.

"Then why don't you tell me? Why did you stop talking to me?"

The ice cubes in Natalie's drink cracked and settled. "What do you want me to say, Annie?"

"I want you to say this isn't happening." Annie's voice grew louder. "I want you to tell me what's really been bothering you so we can work it out together."

"You're yelling," Natalie said calmly.

"Of course I am! I'm upset! Aren't you upset?"

"This isn't easy for me," Natalie said after a long silence.

"Good!" Annie exploded. "You owe me! You owe us!"

"And what about you?" Natalie countered. "What about all the planning you did without telling me."

"You did more than plan," Annie shot back. She lowered her voice. "You can't think it's going to last with Maggie."

"I didn't expect you to understand," Natalie said wearily.

"And just what am I supposed to understand, Natalie? That some trick you fucked is going to know you better than I do? We have a history. Ten years! Doesn't that mean anything to you?"

Natalie dug deeper into her silence and didn't answer.

"Come on, tell me." Annie's face was red, her eyes bore into Natalie.

"I won't talk to you when you're like this."

"Fuck you, Natalie. Fuck you and your hypocritical logic. If you were a man, I'd tell you you were thinking with your dick."

"How many times do I have to tell you?" Natalie yelled in rage and frustration. How much easier to be angry! "You don't understand!"

Annie burst into tears. "Then make me understand, Nat! Explain what's going on, why you're doing this, what happened to us. I don't have to like it, but if it's really right, I'll understand."

"If I try to explain it to you, you'll try to talk me out of it. You'll tell me it's because I'm getting old or I'm overworked or something. I know what I'm doing."

"As your friend, if nothing else, I'm telling you you're wrong."

A feeling of her old love for Annie stabbed toward Natalie, but she was past its reach. "Maybe we're done," she offered lamely. "Maybe our time is coming to an end. Maybe we've gone as far as we were meant to go."

Natalie rose and went into the den, closing the door behind her. She sat at her desk, clamping her hands onto the arms of her chair to steady herself. She wasn't angry, she wasn't calm. She was oddly separate from herself. Over the years she had relied on Annie's instincts whenever she had a problem. If she explained even the most complicated legal situation carefully, Annie could always give her a new perspective on it. Annie's amazing perception was one of the characteristics that had drawn Natalie to her in the first place. Who would she turn to now?

She wasn't aware of how long she'd been sitting

there when Annie knocked on the door. "Come in," she answered.

Annie's eyes were red and swollen from crying. Natalie thought she detected a slight tremor to her hands, but couldn't be sure because Annie jammed them into her jacket pocket as soon as she opened the door. "This will only take a minute." Her voice was calm, so charged with emotion as to seem almost devoid of any. "I'm leaving now, and I don't want you here when I get back. I don't care where you go, but I don't want to hear from you for a while."

Natalie started to say something, but a look from Annie silenced her.

"I'm willing to fight for us, Nat, but not unless you are. If you're stupid enough to want to throw it all away, fine. I won't come chasing after you. But after a certain point I won't let you back, either. So you'd better make damn sure you know what you're doing."

Natalie made no response.

"The hardest thing is, I always thought we were invincible." Annie didn't close the door, she just walked away.

Natalie sat numbly at her desk for a long time, immobilized by conflict: Be there when Annie came back, try to explain; Go to Maggie, that's what you really want. When the phone rang, she was sure it was Annie calling to say she'd be right back. But it was only a woman conducting a survey for the *L.A. Times*. The call got her moving again. She needed to talk to someone. She tried Blair, who was out. She left her message. The numbness had started to wear off and something that was going to be major pain shaped itself around her heart. She went into the bedroom and threw some things into a bag as carelessly as she'd seen people do it on TV, dumping shirts and suits into a suitcase without regard to what they would look like when she wore them. She left another message for Blair before she locked up the house, got in her car, and drove off.

The hotel was one of several lining Ocean Avenue, a wide boulevard across the street from the palisades overlooking the Santa Monica Pier.

Natalie put her new black briefcase beside her on the huge bed, prominently displayed to remind herself who she was. NJB. Those initials and the case were her brand name, her label. They at least told her she was still a lawyer.

Whenever she'd been away from Annie before, she'd had a sense of invisible connection, an unbreakable thread that linked them across any distance. That night she was alone in a way she hadn't been for years, unconnected and adrift. She wanted to call Maggie, but didn't know what to say. She could just show up on her doorstep — that had worked well the first time — but she couldn't face saying out loud, to another person, that she had left Annie.

She had catapulted herself into a world totally foreign to her. One that did not contain Annie. For now this crummy hotel room was her new reality.

Here she was defined only by her possessions. If it wasn't tangible, it didn't exist. By virtue of her suitcase, she knew she existed.

She sat for a long time in the uncomfortable armchair in the darkest corner of the room. Then she paced. Sat again. She had started unpacking but didn't have enough hangers and now her clothes were all over the room — some in the closet, some tossed on the bed, the rest still in the suitcase.

She tried Blair every few minutes, obsessed with reaching her, and left a flurry of messages.

She got through to Maggie, but wouldn't talk more than to tell her she was at a hotel and would call her the next day.

She rang the house, but hung up as soon as the machine came on.

It was unbelievable to her that she hadn't thought about the ramifications of her actions with Maggie. And ironic — her clients hired her to study all aspects of a situation so that she could advise them of their best course of action. Even her developers, men who thrived on risk, were more cautious than she'd been. But she had been powerless against her longing for Maggie — she had seen no alternatives. Or had she succumbed to something that simply translated into longing for Maggie? Was Annie right? Natalie had functioned so long under the aegis of the impostor that it would naturally be difficult to take her first steps on her own.

She sat alone in her rented room. She looked around for the clock to set the alarm for the next morning, but there was none and she hadn't brought hers. Not that she expected to sleep. The enormity of the consequences of her actions was just beginning to permeate the edge of her consciousness, an edge made thick and dull by the sexual haze in which she'd immersed herself.

She tried Blair one last time.

At dinner, Blair was dissatisfied with the food and the service at what was usually one of her favorite restaurants. Her restlessness had nagged her all evening. Only when she and Roxanne were in bed together could Blair begin to settle down. She burrowed into Roxanne to find the closest thing to peace she knew.

She returned home around 2:00 a.m. to several messages from Natalie on her machine. The first was a terse, "Hi, call me later, it's important." Next came, "I have to see you tonight. Call me, no matter what time you get in." She had never heard her friend so agitated. This was the call Blair had been more or less expecting since Natalie's birthday. The last and most frantic message said, "It's one-fifteen. You won't be able to reach me, so I'll call you. . . . No, I'll meet you for breakfast at — no, I'll be at your place by seven-thirty. I'll make breakfast."

Although she had received a lot of SOS calls from friends, this was the first time Natalie or Annie had needed her this urgently.

At three that morning, a helicopter circled the neighborhood, its bass rattling the walls and pounding in Blair's chest. A huge moth battered between the shade and the window. The noises mixed with her thoughts, which were of Natalie and Annie, Ted, and

Lillian. The names circled each other much like the sound from the helicopter. Battered and fluttered inside her mind. And even in her semi-awake state — or maybe her supra-awake state, because she was very aware of each of these things — even then she thought, I am like that juggler I watch, and these are the things I am suspending before myself. She didn't know the why of these particular individuals — why wasn't Constance there? or Paul? — she couldn't see their relationship to each other, or to her. She lay in the dark, searching for connections. Ignorant of her responsibility to each of these people, she knew only that she could not let any of them fall.

Only a few other early morning shoppers roamed the empty supermarket. Natalie wasn't prepared for the special Thanksgiving reminders at the end of each aisle. The elaborate displays of roasting pans and racks, basters, and Pyrex measuring cups only emphasized her peculiar rootless position. She walked by cans of sweet potatoes, pumpkin filling for pies, bags of marshmallows. Just get what you need and get out, she told herself.

Natalie checked the contents of her basket: a half-dozen eggs, a small chunk of goat cheese, a loaf of french bread. Melon would be nice, she thought, or a papaya. Either that or fresh orange juice. In the produce section she was met by the warm summer smell of peaches from New Zealand. Should she get some for Annie? No — she'd forgotten again.

Natalie's surroundings spun around her, a

dizzying blur of brightly colored squash, peppers, the vivid greens of spinach, lettuce, leeks. She reached for the edge of a display case to steady herself.

Stay with the tangible, she reminded herself. Stay in the present. If she relied on her five senses, she'd be okay. She took comfort in the firm waxy heft of the tomatoes. After the chaos of the past forty-eight hours, here at least was something familiar.

An ambulance was parked in front of Blair's building when Natalie arrived. The sun was already strong, and heat waves shimmered off the vehicle. The driver's door and the rear door were open. The radio spat out intervals of static broken by calls and code letters. A few curious neighborhood residents craned over balconies and looked out windows to see what was going on; some had stepped out of the building and were clustered several feet down the sidewalk. They had descended with their coffee mugs. One held a dog on a leash.

The paramedics wheeled their patient out on a gurney. Natalie recognized someone who bore a vague resemblance to Blair's neighbor, Ted. She was stunned at his changed appearance. He'd been sleek. Now he was gaunt.

A wild look in his eyes told Natalie he wasn't fully aware of what was going on around him. He didn't seem to be able to speak. Oblivious to the IV in his thigh, he kept sitting up, trying to make sense out of what was happening. The paramedics told him to lie back, and very loudly explained to him what they were doing and where they were taking him. A man Natalie had met through Blair but whose name she couldn't remember walked alongside the gurney.

Blair must have been out on her run because she came panting up from the beach now. "Oh, my God!" she exclaimed, and immediately went over to Ted's friend and put her arm through his. "Duncan, what happened?"

"I was bringing him his breakfast and found him on the floor. He was having convulsions." He talked to Blair but his eyes followed everything the paramedics did. One of them was now on the radio to the hospital, announcing they were bringing in an AIDS patient, male, around forty years old. "Ted, they're taking you to the hospital." Duncan talked as loudly as the paramedics. "I'll be there." Ted didn't seem to recognize him.

Blair squeezed Duncan's arm. "I'll stop by to see him later."

"Thanks, Blair."

She hugged Duncan before coming back to Natalie.

"I had no idea he'd gotten so sick," Natalie said as they walked upstairs together.

"He was doing very well until just recently."

Natalie sent Blair to shower while she fixed their breakfast. Annie had always liked Ted, and Natalie's first reaction had been to call and tell her what had happened. Reality hit her again — only Blair could call. She herself couldn't call Annie about that or any other incident that might happen during this day or many others to come — and again she experienced a slight dizziness, felt the room spin quietly around her. Focusing on the safe smell of the basil she had just rinsed, she put the remainder of the goat cheese on a little plate.

She didn't have too much trouble finding what she needed in Blair's kitchen, mainly because Blair didn't have too much to look for. When Blair emerged from the bedroom, looking crisp and professional in an off-white shirt and tan slacks, the table on the patio was set, the bread was toasted, coffee made, and Natalie was just folding a golden omelette onto a plate.

"I could get used to this," Blair said as she poured coffee for both of them.

They ate outside. Blair seemed to enjoy her omelette, but Natalie couldn't touch her food.

Spreading cheese on her toast, Blair looked over at Natalie. "You aren't eating."

"I'm not very hungry." Natalie had come to Blair's to make some connection with what had been her real life. She'd envisioned telling Blair everything that had happened, hoping that in the re-telling she'd see what had driven her to do what she'd done. Blair would understand, if anyone would, her impulsive behavior. She'd start with the Halloween party, or even before, when she'd first noticed the jolt she got whenever she saw Maggie. Maybe by explaining the events leading up to the past two days she'd understand her own longing. She'd come here for approval — whether from Blair or her own self, she couldn't yet be sure.

The silence grew awkward. She had to say something. No matter what Blair's suspicions, Blair would never push anyone to talk. Blair was looking at her now, expecting an explanation. Natalie thought: Blair must know something's up, or she wouldn't have made such a point of not asking how I'm doing or why I've been so desperate to come. But she didn't know how to begin. Why was this so hard? Here was, if not approval, at least release. Blair was still looking at her, patiently waiting. Natalie's mouth was dry. She took a sip of coffee. Her hand trembled when she replaced the cup.

"I . . ." No footing. Everything spinning. The life she'd built around her relationship, her future — what had she done? She reminded herself: think tangible, pay attention to your surroundings: the sound of the surf; the only sign of morning fog a lingering haze that muted distant objects. The exercise wasn't working. Her mind still raced. What was Annie doing right now? Had she slept at all? What about Maggie? Would Maggie even want her? Don't — stay here. The sun reflecting on the surface of her coffee, the breeze threatening to carry off her napkin. She put her cup on the napkin to weight it down. Deep breath, long exhalation. Spit it out. "I really fucked up, Blair."

Chapter Ten
Crossing the Line

Annie lay on a chaise in the sun, one arm thrown over her eyes, which were very sensitive from all her crying. Tony was curled in the shade beneath her. On this unseasonably warm day, she wore only running tights and a T-shirt. The CD had finished playing, and she didn't have the energy to get up and put in another one.

She had shut off the answering machine, and the phone had been ringing all morning. She let it ring.

She knew she should have called the office to tell them she wouldn't be in, but even that seemed beyond her power.

When the doorbell rang, she made no move to answer it, merely called out, "Who is it?"

"Leah."

Just what I need, she thought. "The gate's open."

Leah crossed the pool deck. "I've been calling all morning. I can understand anyone wanting to play hooky, but why didn't you call? We were worried about you."

Annie half raised herself to look at Leah. Leah ran the last few steps. "Are you okay?"

"Not really," Annie said.

Someone else's concern was enough to break the tenuous hold she had on her emotions, and she started to cry. She managed to gasp out the basic details — Maggie, Natalie checking into a hotel, her own disorientation — while Leah held her.

When she calmed down, Leah pulled another chair closer to Annie's, and sat near her, stroking her hand.

Cleansed or opened by her cry, Annie felt a rush of words well inside her. They came spilling out, and in her confusion she didn't know whether they made sense, but she was powerless to stop them. "I can understand this, I really can. Or maybe part of me can. Rationally and logically, I can look at this and think I know what's going on." But even as she spoke the words she realized she knew nothing at all. Natalie was her family, her home. Natalie's leaving didn't make any sense. Without Natalie, she had no definition. Natalie was the foundation that made everything else in her life possible.

"I didn't expect anything to really happen, you know? I knew she was unhappy, but she's always stressed out from work. That passes." She ran out of steam, paused. "I never thought she'd go this far." She snorted. "Shows how much I know. I was such a chump. I should have known. I *did* know." She slapped her fist into her belly. "Inside I knew. I just kept believing her when she said it was about work. Or I wanted to believe her. But I knew." She rambled for a long time, often repeating herself, leaving one sentence unfinished in her haste to jump to the next.

Leah listened patiently. "This has more to do with Natalie than with you," she assured her. "All you can do," she advised, "is to keep going. Natalie will come back."

"I'm not sure I want her to." And that thought so overwhelmed Annie that it prompted a new outburst of tears and sobs.

When Annie recovered enough to open her eyes, she noticed Leah was sitting in the same position. She hadn't even taken off her shoes. Little trickles of sweat rolled down her neck, and dark stains were appearing under her arms. "Sorry I'm such a poor hostess," Annie said. "Why don't you take off your shirt and make yourself comfortable."

Leah stayed and made Annie eat lunch before she went back to the office. That evening she returned with food and a bottle of Chardonnay. She grilled chicken and steamed some vegetables and forced Annie to eat.

Annie drank more wine than was usual for her, and was not at all affected by the alcohol. She talked non-stop about Natalie, monitoring every emotion she felt, often grabbing Leah's arm to make a point. Leah listened to her, continued to offer vague reassurances that everything would work out for the best, reminded Annie that her friends were there for support.

Annie didn't want friends. She wanted Natalie.

For the next five nights she ate dinner with Leah. Rather, Leah ate dinner and Annie pushed food around her plate.

Work was out of the question.

Mostly she drove. Up along the coast to Santa Barbara, almost two hours accounted for. Down to San Diego, a longer drive, especially along the ocean. And that was what she needed, the view of the water; its vast expanse soothed her.

At the end of a week of driving, she surprised Leah by saying, "I feel like going dancing."

"I don't believe you," Leah said.

Annie hadn't been to a club in years, was notorious among her friends for her dislike of the scene. But this urge to go out didn't surprise her, any more than putting a thousand miles on her car had.

"Are you sure you're up for this?" Leah asked.

"I want to go somewhere loud where I don't have to think for a few hours." When she put it that way, the idea made sense even to her. "So can we go?"

That Saturday Leah picked her up for dinner. They hadn't driven more than two minutes when Annie leaned over to shut off the radio. "All they play are love songs!" She hadn't had to relate to broken hearts for ten years, hadn't thought about herself or had to monitor her feelings this way. "I never thought I'd have to go through this again."

Annie said as Leah studied her menu, "I think I'll come back to work on Monday. I think I can concentrate enough so that I won't be a liability."

"You know we can cover till you're ready."

"I know."

"Annie, I'm sure this is going to work out," Leah offered tentatively.

"What does that mean?"

"What do you want it to mean?"

"You're beginning to sound like your therapist. Or mine. And I don't want one." Annie didn't mean to be hard on Leah, but she was trying desperately to keep off the topic. Her tone softened, she said, "Let's just have a good time tonight, okay?"

"Fine with me," Leah answered.

Leah checked her watch as they left the restaurant. "We have some time to kill."

"That's one of the reasons we never went dancing," Annie said. "Who wants to wait till eleven or later to arrive in some smoky, loud, dark, depressing place?"

Two hours later Leah navigated them through the crowd to the bar, where she ordered each of them a beer.

"And a shot of Gold on the side," Annie added.

Leah looked at her, surprised.

Annie shrugged. "Tequila makes me dance."

She scanned the crowd. "I don't know what you see in them. Don't they just make you feel old?" She took a long fortifying drink of beer. "Though I'm asking the wrong person. Natalie's the new expert on the attractions of younger women."

That observation drove her to the bar to order another shot. If I'm drinking to cover my pain, she thought, I'm beginning to get some results. The women didn't look quite so young, and the music tempted her. "As long as we're here, we might as well dance," she said, and led Leah out to the floor.

The tequila loosened the block of ice she'd carried inside her, and opened her to the rhythm. As she danced she forgot about Natalie, forgot everything except the beat pounding in her chest. The room didn't feel so strange to her anymore, she remembered the routine, how to use her body in dance, how to talk to a woman without words. But that was no longer appropriate for her. She was married. A wallop of present time, then: Natalie's gone. But if you let the beat inside you, close your eyes . . .

A slow song began. Leah pulled Annie to her, Annie put her arms around Leah's neck, her head on Leah's shoulder. They moved slowly together and Annie almost forgot where she was until the D.J. segued into a fast number. Annie picked up the beat and spun away from Leah.

They stopped dancing long enough to order two more beers. While Leah was paying for them — for some reason, she insisted on treating Annie — a tall young woman who had been eyeing them from the sidelines asked Annie to dance.

Annie returned to Leah after a few songs. She had worked up a sweat and wiped her face with a napkin as Leah held her beer and the bartender pushed another tequila towards her. Annie downed the shot in one gulp, took a swig of beer.

"For someone who's been out of circulation so long, you're a pretty hot ticket," Leah complimented her.

"I'd forgotten how much I love to dance." And that the bars were fun sometimes. All these women, the camaraderie. Why hadn't she and Natalie ever gone?

Leah had a hard time pulling her away when last call was announced.

"How much did you have to drink?" Annie asked when they were in the parking lot.

"I'm okay to drive."

"Good, because I'm not." She tossed Leah the car keys and settled herself in the passenger side. "Phew!" She wrinkled her nose at the strong odor of cigarette smoke permeating their clothes and hair. As they drove away she opened the windows and the sunroof. Cool air filled the car. "This ought to sober us up."

As they drove up the canyon to the house, the air turned even cooler but was extraordinarily fragrant, green and fresh. Annie leaned back against the seat. "That's more like it." She closed her eyes. Opened them almost immediately, clutching her head. Mustn't do that.

"How about a nightcap?" Annie offered. She went to the liquor cabinet and stooped down to retrieve a bottle. Standing, she swayed and lost her balance. Leah caught her before she fell.

"Can't you do anything about keeping this room still?" she asked as Leah steadied her.

"I think maybe we've both had enough," Leah said.

Annie was dimly aware of being steered into the bedroom, stumbling once, being helped onto the bed. She had unbuttoned her shirt, and it hung open now. She was aware, too, of Leah staring at her breasts.

194

Why? She'd seen them countless times, they rarely wore tops around the pool. Well, she'd always suspected that Leah had a crush on her, Natalie had teased about it, and she'd probably known it, too, deep inside.

And now here was Leah, staring at her body. Adoring puppy Leah. Leah who could not get her own life together and had been helping Annie through her mess. Leah who worshipped Natalie and Annie as the model couple. Here was Leah, in her bedroom, undressing her.

The whole idea struck Annie as comical, and she giggled as Leah started to work her pants down over her hips. Leah knelt before her, and Annie stood up to make the job easier. She laid her hands on Leah's shoulders to steady herself, but Leah's tugging threw her off balance, and she plopped back on the bed. "I'm not much help, am I?"

Sitting on the edge of the bed, with Leah kneeling in front of her, they were almost eye level. Annie's pants were down around her knees, her shirt hung open. Leah was very sweet, really, to do this. She put her hand on Leah's cheek, looked into her eyes, and jokingly asked, "However can I repay you for coming to the rescue in my hour of need?"

Leah leaned towards her. The scent of beer was sweet on her breath. "I can think of several ways." Leah put her lips against Annie's.

They kissed, slowly at first. Annie wanted to close her eyes but knew the room would spin so she kept them open. But things were spinning anyway.

What am I doing? she thought. She didn't push Leah away. Leah's hands were all over her. Just when Annie moved to take them from her breasts, they were between her legs. Leah moved with the urgency of someone who sensed this might be snatched from her at any time, and she was going to get as much as she could. Part of Annie wanted to stop what had begun. She was oddly distracted, observed everything with the skewed clarity she possessed only when she'd had too much to drink. She marvelled at the warmth of Leah's skin — and of course that meant she was touching Leah with her distant hands. And Leah was kissing her breasts. Even as she wondered how this had happened and how to stop it, Annie compared the substantial weight of her lover, Natalie's size, to Leah's light touch. And Leah's skin felt completely different from Natalie's.

Annie became aware of another sensation. Leah's thigh pushing between her legs. Oh, too fast now, she thought, this is much too fast. Leah reached down for her, and Annie realized with a shock she was close to coming. Consumed suddenly by a piercing need for Natalie, she writhed away from Leah.

A moment of heavy breathing all around made Annie long to sober up. She wanted real clarity, not what passed for clarity when she was drunk.

Leah was sitting on the edge of the bed, her head in her hands. Annie noticed that Leah's pants were unzipped, her shirt open. She didn't remember any of that. Annie reached out to Leah, touched her hip, reassurance for which of them she wasn't sure.

Annie modestly slipped back into her shirt. "I'm so sorry," she said. "Leah . . ." The name hung there between them, spoken in a tone that was an introduction to further apology, but Annie didn't say anything else.

Without looking at her, Leah broke the long,

charged silence. "Maybe I should leave." She started to rise.

Annie's hand stayed her. "I'm so sorry," she repeated.

Leah stood up. She needed only moderate buttoning and zipping and tucking to make herself presentable again.

"Can I make you some coffee?" Annie offered.

"I'm fine, really," Leah said, without looking at her.

Annie knelt on the bed, gave Leah a chaste kiss on the cheek and started to speak, but what was left to say?

"Try to get some sleep," Leah said before she left the room.

Annie heard the front door close. Heard Leah's car start, then back out of the driveway and accelerate onto the street.

Tony came into the room, putting his head on the bed for attention. "I'm the one who needs it tonight, boy," Annie said, scratching behind his ear. He licked her hand.

That's when she started to cry. She relaxed into her tears, knowing they were her only entrance to sleep.

Chapter Eleven
Close Encounter

The crowds would show up early today, Blair thought as she opened all the windows in the house on Sunday morning. The beautiful weather would attract even the most resolute stay-at-homes. Including herself. She put aside her list of things to do around the house and walked down to a nearby café and sat outside for breakfast and a few sections of the Sunday paper.

She walked home past a teenager slumped on a

bench, cowering behind a posterboard sign printed with her story. She was from a small town outside Boston, it read, had come to L.A. with her boyfriend who had dumped her, and now she needed $136.50 for bus fare home. Blair remembered that Ted had given the kid a quarter a few weeks earlier.

A few hundred yards further down the boardwalk, a scrawny young woman singer with no presence and less voice positioned herself behind the protective barricade of her sound system, inflicting her voice but not her body on the people who passed.

Some performers attracted huge crowds, but others, such as this singer, drew only small clumps of people. Venice welcomed them all; the sun shone and the day was glorious. Blair whistled as she walked. This was a day made for wasting — lingering over the paper, to hell with her busy plans. She was perfectly content to spend it alone, or with any of her friends who might drop in unexpectedly. The only thing she knew for sure was that she'd be out when Paul called.

Her brother had taken to giving her weekly reports ever since he'd taken their mother in to live with him and his family. As if it weren't enough that Blair had to listen to these updates, Paul had some bee in his bonnet about having the family together for Thanksgiving.

Puttering around the house later, half-heartedly trying to make herself do some work, Blair was not totally surprised when Annie rang her buzzer. She'd figured it was only a matter of time before she heard Annie's side of the story.

Holding her head, Annie groaned as she entered the living room. "Now I remember why I don't drink tequila anymore." She walked stiffly and slowly, as if the slightest movement would jar something loose.

"You look like you could use a Bloody Mary."

Annie grimaced. "Is that a joke?"

"I thought maybe a little hair of the dog —"

"Bite your tongue. I don't even want to be reminded of the dog." Annie gingerly lowered herself onto the couch. "I just needed to borrow your view for a while."

Blair settled in a chair on the other side of the coffee table. Annie made uncharacteristic small talk, rattling on about everything except Natalie. Blair didn't push for more, figuring her friend would open up when she was ready. They moved out onto the balcony to watch the assortment of Sunday beachgoers, and observed the cavalcade in silence for a few minutes.

She looked over at Annie then and saw that she was crying silently. Blair moved closer to her, put her arm around Annie's shoulders. "It's hard, I know." Annie turned then, burrowed into Blair, crying and shaking.

Drawing away, Annie sniffed as she rummaged through her pockets for a tissue. "I could kill Natalie for this."

"For what it's worth, this isn't easy for her, either."

"She has the advantage of doing what she wanted to do. Or what she thought she wanted to do." Annie laughed sharply.

"Have you talked to her?" Annie shook her head no. "Are you going to?"

200

"Not for a while. Not until she figures out what she wants."

"What do you want?"

Annie leaned on the railing and studied the crowd below as if she were reading tea leaves for a prediction. "I wish I knew."

"These things have a way of resolving themselves," Blair began, grateful when Annie cut off her bromidic advice mid-sentence.

"These things have a way of screwing up your life," Annie commented dryly. "And the lives of your friends," she continued, not looking Blair in the eye as she related her tale of the previous evening with Leah. "Some resolution that would have been."

Blair couldn't imagine Annie and Leah together, even for a night. But, under the circumstances, she felt Annie was entitled. "Aren't you allowed to get something you need?"

"Yes, but with Leah that's crossing a line better left uncrossed. Besides, I still think of myself as a married woman." Annie gazed out at the view. "Even if I didn't, I'd rather have my friends as friends, not lovers."

"I'm sure Leah understands."

"I hope so. I can't face her yet. I was on my way over there but chickened out. I acted almost as stupidly as Natalie."

Annie sat in almost the exact spot Natalie had occupied when she'd talked about Maggie. Blair wouldn't interrupt unless asked to. She'd learned long ago that people just need to talk, and didn't always want to hear what anyone else had to say. "It's not that I don't blame her at all," Annie said about Maggie, "but she's young. Natalie's older, accomplished, powerful, not to mention good-looking. An attractive combination. Natalie knew what was going on.

"Besides," Annie dismissed Maggie with a wave of her hand, "Maggie, Margie, whoever. I know she's not the issue. And don't say that's mature of me. I've had fantasies of kicking down her door and entering with guns blazing."

"So, what next?"

"I don't know. I don't know when the communication broke down. That's what scares me."

Blair was used to her friends splitting up. It was always just a matter of time, and never made much difference in the long run. Everyone became friends again sooner or later. But Annie and Natalie's break-up was big news in the community. Already Blair had received lots of calls, Have you heard, Is it true. Word was out and the phone lines were buzzing. No one could believe it. And yet, because of the nature of their relationship, no one was willing to dismiss them as another casualty. Their relationship was viewed as a marriage, not an affair.

"I'm trying to figure out my part in this, what I did wrong."

"Maybe this is just Natalie's shit," Blair offered.

"Maybe. It's so strange without her. We don't even talk. I've spoken to her secretary a few times — mostly to cancel social engagements. All the little pieces of our life that Natalie chose to ignore so she could recapture her youth or whatever the fuck she's trying to do." The spark of anger in her voice ignited in her eyes, and she turned to Blair, as if everything were her fault. "And I'm supposed to wait patiently until she realizes she wants to come home?"

The ringing phone saved Blair from having to reply. She didn't have to get up to answer it, but when she heard the first tentative "Sis?" she went inside.

Paul mumbled, "Everyone I talked to said it was the best place. I don't know, though," he stammered, "it was the hardest thing I'd ever had to do."

He was telling her he'd put Constance in a home. Years of anger at her brother washed away when Blair heard the anguish in his voice as he described leaving Constance in a strange new room. "You did the right thing, Paul. She was only getting worse, you said so yourself, and that wasn't fair to Susan and the kids."

"Maybe you could come up early for Thanksgiving, we could visit her."

Blair almost considered accepting the invitation. He seemed to sincerely want her there, to need her presence. "I've got plans here."

"Friends aren't the same as family," Paul said.

Blair knew there was no way to explain to him that some of her friends were family.

When Blair stepped back outside, Annie had settled into the *New York Times* she'd brought with her. Blair thumbed through the magazine section. She didn't talk about her family with anyone, except for joking references to Paul's homophobia. No one knew about her mother's condition, and this wasn't the time to burden Annie with it.

The reality of Paul's action hadn't sunk in yet. How could it — she hadn't spoken to or seen Constance for such a long time, how could she be expected to absorb the news? The only part of Paul's description she'd recognized was Constance's excellent physical condition. Except for the lump in her breast, their mother hadn't been sick a day in her life. What would it be like to see her now, looking healthy as a horse but incapable of taking care of herself? Blair couldn't imagine.

Annie had fallen asleep in her chair. She stirred now, slowly opened her eyes to announce that she was feeling much better. "This is the happiest my hangover's been all day. Thank you, Blair. I guess I can't put Leah off any longer. Wish me luck."

Blair walked Annie to the door. Before leaving Annie turned back to her and said, "Don't let her do anything too stupid, okay, Blair?"

"I wish it were up to me, kiddo."

Blair decided to skip her run that day and go to the hospital to see Ted. She had showered, and was finishing dressing when the phone rang. "Hey Duncan, I was just getting ready to come over. Tell Ted he's missing a great day. All his favorites are out."

"Blair . . ."

With a lurch in the pit of her stomach she knew why he was calling.

"He died about five this morning. He was very peaceful towards the end."

Another piece of information she was incapable of processing. "I bought him a goofy T-shirt." As if that would change anything. "Is there anything I can do?"

Duncan said he had been on the phone all day,

contacting Ted's parents in Iowa and arranging the funeral. "If you know anyone who might want to come . . ."

"I'll call them."

"Thanks." The service would be Wednesday, with a reception afterwards at Ted's place. Blair said she'd be there.

She was numb when she hung up. Her first instinct was to minimize her sense of loss. She hadn't been that close to Ted, really, he'd been a very small part of her life. But she felt an empty space that she kept returning to, the way you worry a tooth that hurts. She was aware suddenly of his apartment yawning empty next to hers. (After her father died, she'd felt his presence everywhere, once had even picked up the phone to call him. But she hadn't known Ted that well, this should be different. She shrugged off the ghosts tugging at her memory.) What happened to her glorious, lazy day? She needed to get out now, and decided to go for her run.

Usually she waited for the weekend crowds to leave before reclaiming her stretch of beach. It was too easy to get caught up in the visual commotion, she'd forget to look at the water. She'd run at this hour with Ted a few times. He liked to start off through the crowds, proud of the body he worked so hard to maintain, enjoying the appreciative looks he got from other men.

Let this be in honor of Ted, Blair thought, and gave an extra kick to her stride.

She ran towards Windward Avenue, having to slow almost to a walk to negotiate through the crowds wreathed around the most popular performers.

The commotion was too much for her today, even

in Ted's honor. The constant bombardment made her turn off when she reached Windward, away from the water. She headed into the back streets of Venice, Ted foremost in her thoughts. Several times in his last months he'd asked, "What's it all about, Blair?" Sometimes, on good days, when he was feeling strong and confident, he'd sing it to the tune of "Alfie." The question was rhetorical then, the answer didn't matter as long as he was feeling okay and was still alive. Just the other day in the hospital, hooked up to I.V. drips and in a great deal of pain, he asked again, this time needing an answer. Blair wasn't used to having serious conversations with him, and was a little taken aback by his frankness. He wasn't afraid to be intimate with anyone anymore, saw no risk in saying what he felt. Blair, inadequate to his challenge, had no answers for him.

She picked up her pace, hoping to outrun these demons that chased her.

Once off the main drags, she ran towards the canals. She jogged on a quiet little street, over the rise and fall of bridges wide enough to allow passage of one car. The houses that lined the canals were an eclectic mix of funky little shacks, California bungalows, and modern glass and stone boxes. An assortment of canoes and rowboats were tied up to docks in many of the backyards.

A thought kept nagging at her: I'm supposed to be somewhere else. Then she remembered: Oh yes, visiting Ted in the hospital. She never got to say good-bye to him. A helpless feeling slowed her trot to a walk.

Pausing at a tiny park at the foot of a bridge, she watched a father and his little daughter feeding the ducks that flocked to this water bird sanctuary. The child, delighted and afraid at the same time as she offered the ducks bread, ran screaming and terrified back to her father when the birds approached to accept her offering.

He was very patient with her. As Blair watched, the burly man squatted down and his daughter nestled snugly against him as they fed the ducks together. Sheltered by her father's strong arms and body, the little girl became much more reckless and daring. If a duck came too close, all she had to do was squirm backwards an inch to be totally protected.

Blair couldn't remember the last time she'd felt that sense of absolute safety.

Ted's funeral was quite simple. The service was an improvement over others Blair had attended, where the clergyman droned on about a perfect stranger. This minister knew Ted, and after brief introductory remarks introduced three of his friends who told stories about Ted. One fellow activist talked about Ted's political concerns. A co-worker shared a story about Ted's first day on the job. Duncan spoke last. As Blair was drawn into their tales, she expected to turn and catch Ted's reaction to a particularly funny incident, or his blush at some of the lavish praise.

The minister was asking the mourners to join with him in reciting the Lord's prayer. Blair kept her eyes on Ted's casket, offering not a prayer but an answer finally to his question. The answer had been there all along, she wanted to tell him. It was the way he'd lived his life, generous and caring; it was obvious in the love and respect returned to him by his friends and colleagues.

Back at her place, she flopped down on the couch, exhausted. She thought of her waking dream about juggling. Now, clearly, she had too many balls in the air at once. Ted was gone. Her mother, distant for years, was now completely inaccessible. Natalie and Annie were split up. What had happened to her world?

In the emotion of the past days she'd forgotten to cancel dinner with Roxanne for that night. They went to a Thai restaurant, and over bottles of Amarit Blair found herself talking a lot about Ted. She recounted incidents she wasn't aware of remembering. The time she'd loaned him some clothes for a drag party. How much healthier her plants looked when she came back from a trip because he'd taken better care of them than she ever did. She was at the number of small details she remembered. Even more surprised to be telling them to Roxanne. "Sorry I'm dumping all this on you," she said.

"I'm glad you're telling me."

"Why?"

"Maybe it means you trust me a little."

Blair didn't think trust had anything to do with it. She'd just been to the guy's funeral, after all. But she kept talking. She didn't understand anything anymore. She told Roxanne about Natalie and Annie's break-up. And about Constance. "It's like someone decided things were going too well, so let's shake it up a little. A lot." Blair paused, embarrassed. "I don't know why I'm telling you all this."

Having broken her own spell, she changed the subject and nothing Roxanne said could induce her to return to it.

But that night, for the first time, Blair invited Roxanne back to her place.

She looked forward to sex with her, to escaping to the one place she always understood. They began with long, deep kisses. Blair slowly eased herself down Roxanne's body. But this time Roxanne would be the initiator. Rolling herself on top of Blair, "Lie back," she directed, "let me start."

Roxanne moved slowly over Blair's body, hands and mouth constantly exploring or, encouraged by Blair's increasing arousal, lingering in one spot.

Blair reached between Roxanne's legs, felt how wet she was, began slow strokes that caused Roxanne to let out a low moan before she pulled away to kneel over Blair. "I'm not that easily distracted," Roxanne said, resuming her exploration. Tracing her fingers over Blair's lips, "You're very beautiful," she said.

Embarrassed, Blair pulled Roxanne to her. But Roxanne wouldn't be held. She started to edge herself down between Blair's legs. "No, stay here."

"I want my mouth on you," Roxanne whispered. "Please."

"Blair. Please." Who was that, Roxanne or Hallie?

Blair lay back and closed her eyes. Just as years ago that massage from Hallie had released images stored in her muscles, so now Roxanne's mouth and tongue were the key that unlocked memory and feeling. She saw again, or sensed, that room within herself. It was still warm and filled with light, but no longer empty. Ted was there, healthy and sound, smiling the way he did after beating her in a sprint at the end of a run. Her father stood nearby, smiling also, holding out his arms to Blair. Flicks of Roxanne's tongue triggered appearances by her mother, dressed for an outing to the museum, and her father, grilling steaks on a summer night. Even Natalie and Annie were there, Hallie, too — all these people summoned somehow by what Roxanne was doing to her.

Determined to stop the barrage of ghosts, Blair reached for Roxanne, to pull her up, to make love to her, but Roxanne was unyielding, her mouth on Blair insistent. There was nothing to do but shut her eyes tighter against the ghosts, dive down deeper to avoid them, past the place of words, to where there was only feeling. Blair grabbed Roxanne's head and held it fast as she moved and jerked not into oblivion but into such a clarity of thought that she surfaced wildly from its depths, gasping for air, and heaving great gulping sobs.

Afterward, she thought she wanted to pull away from Roxanne, but let herself be held for a long time.

That night, she was visited by her mother. Blair was pasting words and pictures into a scrapbook. She looked up and saw her mother, dressed to go out, standing in the doorway. Constance wore a full-length white and grey fur coat — not one she'd ever owned, this belonged to the dream — over a black evening dress. Blair took in her mother's appearance, approved, and said casually, "You smell good." She had already turned back to her scrapbook when she realized that she wasn't going to see her mother again. As she quickly rose and crossed the room to her, a slip of paper with the word ANGER written on it floated out of her hand onto the floor. She picked it up quickly, not so much to hide it from her mother, but because it wasn't a big issue anymore, just something that belonged in the scrapbook. She put her arm around her mother, drew herself close, and laid her head on her mother's shoulder. The coat's fur was thick, slightly coarse and soft at the same time. Blair was enveloped in her mother's aroma — perfume, powder, the slight musty smell of the coat. "I miss you, Mommy," she said, and started to cry.

She woke up. Her face was wet. Where had all these tears come from? She couldn't shake the dream, nor was she completely comfortable thinking of it as a dream. Her mother's presence had been so real that Blair woke smelling her perfume. Or was that Roxanne's scent lingering on her hands and body? She got out of bed, put on a robe, and walked downstairs. She stepped out onto the balcony, hoping the cold air would clear her head.

She was inside out, all her feelings exposed, clinging to her skin.

Normally her time, this four a.m. felt dramatically different to her, foreign. She derived no power from the dark. For once she was glad that someone was asleep upstairs. The night was perfectly still. No incidental noises from cars, dogs, or neighbors. Only the distant and steady pounding of the surf, crashing and receding, crashing and receding.

Chapter Twelve
Emergencies

Maggie studied during breakfast. Natalie read the morning paper in silence, a totally unnatural condition for her. She was used to shouting back at headlines, incensed by injustices committed by any number of enemies — right-to-lifers, televangelists or fundamentalists, hard-line conservative Republicans, any of the good ole boys. Annie would jump right in with her. They often solved a lot of the world's problems before going off to work.

Natalie wanted to read something to Maggie, but thought better of it when she saw the scowl of concentration on her face as she highlighted paragraphs in her textbook.

Inspired by the uncluttered, dedicated life Maggie lived, Natalie had been able to clear away much of the backlog of work that had accumulated at the office. Stripped of all the extraneous responsibilities of living in her house, she developed a spartan — not to be confused with celibate — routine. Despite the cramped quarters, she worked at Maggie's apartment on weekends — marathon sessions interrupted only by meals and incredible, mind-clearing sex.

Her new routine bore no resemblance to her old one. Maggie wouldn't even take time for Thanksgiving. Natalie was going to roast a turkey for Maggie and her study group. "Let's not make too big a deal of it, we've got a lot of con law to cover," was Maggie's response to Natalie's offer. Not making a big deal was fine with Natalie. She didn't think she could handle too many reminders of what she would have been doing had she been with Annie.

Not that she was able to push it completely out of her mind. She was lugging around ten years worth of reminders. Sometimes they were too much for her and she cried. If this happened when she was with Maggie, Maggie would comfort her. The comforting inevitably turned to lovemaking. They didn't talk much, but that was okay, too.

Absorbed in working the crossword puzzle (one of Annie's habits she'd appropriated), Natalie spread jam on her toast. Just as she was about to take a bite, Maggie reached over to her. "You spilled," she said, and wiped away a red drop on Natalie's shirt.

"Shit, this was my last clean blouse." Natalie got up to run cold water on a towel and dab at the stain before it set.

"Allow me." Maggie joined her at the sink, began unbuttoning the blouse.

"I don't have time for this now," Natalie protested.

"For what?" Maggie, all innocence, asked. "I'm just trying to make you presentable." She kissed Natalie's neck as she removed her blouse.

Half an hour later, presentable but very late, Natalie was in her car headed for the office.

This whole crazy time with Maggie she'd wondered if she were living every married person's fantasy: a wild affair with someone young and sexy. Things she thought she'd forgotten, that she thought she'd outgrown, were suddenly a part of her life again: staying up all night making love and talking; episodes like the one this morning, starting out innocently enough and ending up in bed. Even the adolescent excitement of necking was returned to her — after take-out Chinese food their second night together they'd been sitting on Maggie's couch watching the news and suddenly they were kissing and going at each other and coming before they could take off their clothes.

Natalie glanced into the cars around her, studying her fellow commuters, wondering for the first time what their secrets might be. How many of them were living out their dreams, how many just going along, same as always?

Maybe she just had too much invested in her actions and needed to validate them, but she believed that Maggie was restoring elements long missing from her life. Humor. Enthusiasm. Purpose. As far away as they seemed now, her goals upon entering law school had been noble. Her vision of the world and her mission in it had been genuine. Over the years that vision had been clouded over and eroded by reality, by compromise, by the sheer volume of work she'd taken on. She'd struggled lately without any unifying ethic, other than finishing one project so she could catch up on the next. In the back of her mind she accused herself of selling out, becoming a hack.

Maggie's belief in her spurred Natalie on, Maggie's enthusiasm inspired her, renewed some of her old vision. Maggie fired her up. She confided some of this to Blair. "She keeps me honest. It's been a long time since I've felt so vital."

Through Maggie, glimpses of her old self were coming back to her, if only short takes. She still couldn't sleep at night, but that was to be expected, what with all the changes. She wasn't used to the emotional highs and lows of the past few weeks — the constant stress was taking its toll. So was the almost non-stop sex, in bed at night and in the morning, plus impromptu couplings like the one that had taken place earlier. Which reminded her that she'd have to rearrange her schedule to allow another run to the house for clothes — especially blouses.

That blouse she'd stained was one of her favorites, she liked to wear it for important meetings. It had always brought her luck. Today she was having lunch with Matthew Madison, aka The Statue. She had a plan to get Parker Sherman out of her hair. She knew he wouldn't go away, but she could handle him, as long as she watched her back. Without her lucky blouse, well, she'd just have to rely on her good looks and charm. She smiled to herself.

She felt good. She felt renewed. A hundred inconsequential thoughts jammed her head. What a relief after all the heaviness since leaving Annie. A great weight fell from her and the sun illuminated all the possibilities ahead. Out of the corner of her eye she noticed the woman in the next car applying lipstick. Behind her was a super-macho guy in his skeletal Jeep, radio pumping loudly. Maybe I should get one of those, Natalie thought. The partners would flip. She'd bought her Mercedes with their whole-hearted approval. What would they think if she came tearing up in a bright red Renegade?

She was still smiling at the image when the first twinge hit her. It subsided, and she dismissed it as indigestion. But the second, a searing pain in her chest, and the third, accompanied by the racing of her heart, were impossible to ignore.

Traffic, though moving at a steady forty miles an hour, was heavy, so she couldn't change lanes or slow down or speed up. Her palms were sweaty. She wiped each one on her skirt before placing it back on the wheel. The pain came again, a vise tightening around her sternum. It scared her. This was crazy. Hoping to distract herself, she turned up the radio. Her left arm tingled, the fingers on that hand were numb. She took a deep breath. Another sharp stab. She opened all the windows and the sunroof and gulped air into her lungs. Only two more exits and she could get off. Calm down, you're almost there, was the message she relayed to her brain. But it wasn't being received. It was being cut off at her shoulders, by steel fingers pinching into her flesh. This isn't happening. She broke out in a cold sweat and her pulse raced. She was breathing in short shallow gulps that gave her less and less oxygen. God, the pain!

It had its own voice now, an ephemeral sensation buried inside her, a hoarse whisper rasping, "You're not young anymore, serious things happen." But this wasn't about age. This was death speaking to her now. A reminder of death that travelled down her arm and around her chest. No noise from the outside world came to her. She was sealed off in a silent bad dream punctuated only by the pounding of her heart. And when it got so loud that it shut out all other sounds — the traffic, the blasting radio — a chant welled inside her: *AnnieAnnieAnnieAnnieAnnie.* A mantra into which she channelled the only two things she knew at that moment: fear and her will to live. *Annie.*

Her vision narrowed. Through its dark tunnel she headed for her doctor's office. Only with difficulty could she sit up straight.

Her bright thoughts scattered, blasted apart by the fear and pain. With breathtaking clarity she knew only this was real now.

Through and despite her panic she was stunned by the simplicity of her next thought. Something was missing from her life, something only she had the power to adjust. *I can do whatever I want.* Her mind raced into the future. She didn't have to practice law. She could open a restaurant. They could sell the house, get out from under that hill. She could take a sabbatical from work, they could travel. Anything was possible. Bargaining chips stacked up, offerings for Annie.

Her mantra had its own rhythm now, kept perfect time with her racing heartbeat. The piercing empty space inside her — the void that no amount of work or sex with Maggie could fill — was almost bursting with the sound. For the first time in her life Natalie knew what she wanted. For the first time in her life she wasn't sure if she would be able to have it.

No more thoughts now. Her panicky gasps supplied less and less oxygen. Only a fierce will to survive propelled her.

She got off the freeway and drove through busy morning streets, zigzagging around buses and slower cars, leaning on her horn. (*AnnieAnnieAnnieAnnie Annie.*) The pain was constant now, searing. Her pulse was racing, and she was panting, unable to catch her breath. Drenched in a cold sweat then chilled, she was constantly wiping her hands in order to grip the wheel.

She screeched into the parking lot. Not bothering to close the car door, she barged into the building.

The cool pastel waiting room was quiet. A pregnant woman sat calmly reading a book, another patient thumbed through a magazine. Natalie rushed to the reception desk. She'd been coming here for years and knew everyone in the office. "Carrie, I've got to see Irene right away. I'm having a heart attack."

Lillian Webb had been sitting awfully close today, once or twice letting her leg brush against Blair's. They had met in the conference room because it was bigger than Blair's office and she needed the space to spread out her drawings. But Lillian — who had mentioned several times that her husband was out of town — was never more than a few feet away.

Blair had begun to think that Lillian Webb presented the most convenient and expedient solution to the problem of Roxanne. Though it was against her better judgement, Blair needed a quick fix, and Lillian Webb was going to provide it.

She should never have let Roxanne spend the night. Roxanne had said afterward that she felt so much *closer* to Blair. Blair had had trouble fending her off. Roxanne liked her, Roxanne wanted to get more serious. Roxanne was willing to go on as before, but thought there was more between them than causal and occasional sex, that even Blair on some level had to recognize that.

Blair didn't think she had to recognize anything. All she knew was that she was sorry she had cried in front of Roxanne. That's when all this started. Until then, she'd been having a good time. Now she was going to have to do something about it.

She hadn't spent a full night with Roxanne since, which was a good thing because she'd continued to dream about Constance. And wakened crying after each dream. Not because the dreams were bad. On the contrary, in them she had long talks with her mother, made up for years of estrangement. In one dream, Blair introduced Constance to all her friends, even Roxanne.

Lillian leaned over Blair's shoulder to point at something on the board in front of them. Her elegant perfume was enticing, the slight pressure of her arm against Blair's encouraging. Blair shifted closer to Lillian. Why hadn't she thought of this sooner?

Lillian would handle their affair professionally. Just as Blair was about to suggest the possibility of drinks at the Bel Air, she was paged over the intercom. She picked up the phone at the end of the conference table, turning her back on Lillian for privacy.

She said hello several times before she heard her brother's almost unrecognizable voice. "It's all my fault, Blair, I shouldn't have put her in that place." He sounded frantic.

"Slow down, Paul. What's your fault?"

"This wouldn't have happened if I'd kept her with us."

"Paul, what's going on?"

"Mom had a stroke. It's my fault."

Blair did her best to calm her brother. She made him give her the information about where Constance was, the name of her doctor. She managed to learn that Constance had suffered a massive stroke. Her brain stem was intact. "What does that mean, Paul?"

"She's got all her functions, she's breathing on her own. But there's no hope of recovery."

Blair leaned heavily on the table for support after she hung up. The news had knocked the wind out of her. She tried to gather thoughts which were scattered over years and months, mixing up her childhood with last week with eight years ago. Riding serene over the tangle was that image of her mother from the dreams — calm, competent, dressed and perfumed. Blair couldn't fit that image into the confines of a hospital bed.

She became aware then of someone standing close by, not touching her, but near enough to generate sensation. Lillian. Blair had lost sense of her surroundings. Lillian gently placed her hand on Blair's arm. "Are you all right?"

"My mother's sick. I have to go to San Francisco."

Chapter Thirteen
Loose Ends

"How are you doing?" Irene Fields, Natalie's friend and doctor, watched Natalie with concern.

"Better." Natalie took one last deep breath into the paper bag. Her recycled air smelled brown and damp. She popped the bag before handing it to Irene. Her "heart attack" had been hyperventilation brought on by anxiety. The worst was over. She was regaining the feeling in her hands and feet, the tingling had subsided.

"If you thought you were having a heart attack, why didn't you go to a hospital?"

Natalie buttoned her shirt with thick, clumsy fingers. The Valium must be kicking in, she thought. "You're my doctor."

"I'm your gynecologist. Hearts are not exactly my specialty." As they talked, Irene checked Natalie's pulse. "Much better," she said. She turned and picked up the phone. "What's Anne's work number?"

An alarm tried to sound in Natalie's head. "What for?"

"To tell her what happened and to come get you."

"At this stage she'd probably be disappointed it was only an anxiety attack." Natalie had already given Irene a tearful summary of what her last few weeks had been like.

"She wouldn't want to know about this?"

Natalie just shook her head and lay back, shut her eyes. That was as adamant as she could be with her mind softening under the drug. And yet even through the haze, as she thought about Annie she felt an echo of her earlier panic, a muffled reminder.

"Well, tell me who I should call, then."

Natalie didn't feel like seeing or talking to anyone. "I could just rest here till I'm okay to drive."

Irene did not consider this an option.

"All right, all right," Natalie was forced to concede. She gave Irene Maggie's number. She grasped the receiver and brought it to her ear as Irene punched the numbers.

Maggie answered on the fourth ring. "I was just on my way out the door."

223

"You've got class, I told Irene that," Natalie said thickly, her eyes closed.

"You sound weird, where are you?"

Natalie briefly told Maggie what had happened. "I can just take a cab if you don't want to miss class." Maggie, concerned, said she'd be there as soon as possible. Natalie passed the receiver to Irene, who gave Maggie the address before hanging up.

"Don't lecture me," Natalie said flatly.

"Did I say anything?"

"You don't have to."

"I'm just concerned about your health. What you do to your marriage is none of my business. Though as your friend —"

"Just be my doctor right now, okay?" Shouldn't snap at Irene, she gave me the Valium, Natalie smiled to herself. She felt an enforced calm settle over her. Through her fog she heard Irene's voice from very far away.

"Has anything like this happened to you before?"

Natalie remembered the drive back from Palm Springs, that other car swerving across the freeway, her wildly beating heart. "Never like this."

"A couple days off would be in order. Do you think you need any more Valium?" Natalie shook her head. "Good."

"I'll be fine," Natalie said. "Nothing that a little psychotherapy wouldn't cure, right?" She smiled sheepishly.

"Or maybe just a long walk on the beach. With Annie." Irene scrawled a few more notes before closing Natalie's chart. "You can just rest in here till your friend comes. And take it easy." Irene stopped in the doorway. "Natalie, as your doctor, let me just say forty isn't the end of the world."

It's not about that! Natalie wanted to say. Or maybe she did say it. She wasn't sure what was a thought and what actually came out of her mouth. She tried to sit up before Irene left, but a wave of dizziness held her down. She resented Irene's patronizing attitude. This had nothing to do with turning forty.

So then what had brought her here?

The drug kept her from connecting with her memories. Everything was confused, but she thought she remembered crying, telling Irene about Maggie. I'm a mess, she thought. All disheveled, shirt out and unbuttoned, sleeve pushed up for the IV they'd started (just in case it really had been a heart attack). She lay on the table in the chilly examining room, humbled and embarrassed by her experience, grateful for the blanket the Valium had thrown over her mind.

She opened her eyes to Maggie leaning over her. "Are you all right?" Maggie looked worried.

"I'm fine. Irene gave me a Valium."

"Think you're ready to go?"

Natalie slowly sat up, then gingerly swung her legs over the side of the table. She braced herself on the edge a moment before stepping down. Maggie stood close to her, ready to support her if necessary. Natalie swayed, steadied herself, then fumbled into her shoes. "Sorry you had to miss class."

"That's not important."

"I wouldn't have called if Irene hadn't insisted. You can just drop me at the hotel."

"Hey, don't worry, I want to stay with you."

They left Maggie's car in the parking lot, and Maggie drove the Mercedes. Natalie's perceptive mechanisms were off. She didn't seem to be registering temperature or time. Events happened at a great distance from her. A motorcyclist swerved in front of the car, Maggie slammed on the brakes, cursed him. Natalie barely heard her.

"Is this too much?" Maggie asked, opening the sun roof and all the windows.

It must be warm out, Natalie realized. It certainly was very bright, she knew, her eyes weren't adjusting properly, things were overexposed. She let her lids flutter down. Ah, better.

"We're here." Maggie opened the door for her.

Natalie walked unsteadily up the stairs to her room. She rested against the wall as Maggie fiddled with the key. The sun felt good on her face. "I could go to sleep right here."

"Well, hang on one more second," Maggie said, opening the door.

Natalie crawled under the covers Maggie drew back for her. She dropped immediately into a dreamless sleep.

She woke to see Maggie pacing the room restlessly. She closed her eyes again, said, "Why don't you just go to class."

Maggie stopped at the foot of the bed. "Forget class. How are you feeling?"

Natalie made a quick evaluation: attached to the bed; too heavy to move; almost hung over. She answered: "I don't know yet."

Maggie approached the bed, perched tentatively at its foot. "Want me to bring you lunch?"

Natalie hated being an invalid. She didn't want Maggie taking care of her.

She managed to get up, splashed some water on her face. They went out to a coffee shop. They made artificial conversation, circling the topic of Natalie's health and state of mind. She got Maggie started on a one-sided discourse on how things were going at work. She needed time to think. (Annie wouldn't have fallen for that trick. Maggie seemed so young. Her enthusiasm was genuine, but naive, inexperienced. She made everything sound so simple.)

"How about going back to the room?" Maggie asked as they waited for the check. "I could hold you while you sleep."

This whole time with Maggie Natalie had lived with a false euphoria, driven by a desperate need to be right and to have their affair mean something. Despite denying it to Annie — and to herself — she had been blinded by sex with Maggie, tiring almost at once of the walnut shampoo, the tight living quarters, Maggie's youth, even of the sex. She was startled when she admitted to herself how quickly her desire had been slaked. "I'm okay, really. Why don't I take you back to your car."

"Are you sure you're all right?"

Natalie's head was still shrouded, but she needed to be alone. She drove Maggie to Irene's parking lot.

"I'll see you later?" Maggie made it a question.

Natalie hesitated. "Let me see how I feel. I'll call you."

She leaned over and brushed Maggie's cheek with her lips. Not really a kiss.

She went back to the hotel and took a shower. She was extra diligent with her lotion and perfume. She chose her clothes carefully, and couldn't remember how long it had been since she'd dressed for Annie. She hadn't brought that much with her, but she tried all of it on, even the business suits, even though she knew they wouldn't be right. Nothing looked right. She settled finally on comfortable khaki pants and a loose white shirt, and sneakers. A look in the mirror showed her a tall woman in easy, casual clothes. No statement being made. She laughed at the memory of how she'd looked in that bulky jacket she'd bought just after she'd met Maggie. That phase was over now. No more trying to be something or someone she wasn't.

As she drove up the driveway, she felt she was seeing their house for the first time. The tiny front lawn bordered by agapanthus and camellias, the pittosporum so fragrant when in flower. In some ways this felt no different to her than when she drove home every day from work. But she was very careful to park in the driveway, like a guest.

She heard Tony bark his greeting as soon as she got out of the car. He was wild to see her, deliriously spinning around and jumping up and wagging his tail. He rushed to get a ball she threw up the hill for him, chasing after it as she let herself into the house.

She had never associated any particular smell with the house, but now that she'd been away for even these few weeks she walked in and was immediately engulfed in its familiar scents. Not just perfume, but hints of freshly brewed coffee and bath soap and Annie. Natalie walked through the house with a rising sense of wonder. Parts of herself were still here — traces of energy, even, echoes of breaths and heartbeats.

The kitchen counter was littered with toast crumbs. Annie's coffee mug sat in the sink. Soaking in it was the knife she must have used to butter the toast. Natalie smiled at the image of Annie leaning against the counter, sipping her coffee, toast in hand, looking through the morning paper. Annie wouldn't sit for breakfast unless Natalie was around.

As Natalie looked, she sensed a vague change everywhere. Something was different, but what? She moved through the house in search of clues.

The den seemed untouched since she'd last been in it. Everything was as she had left it: the papers on the desk, a file she'd been looking for at the office, law journals and a stack of bills that needed paying. This room smelled different than the others where Annie's scent lingered faintly in the air.

Natalie walked into the bedroom. Annie hadn't made the bed. Half of it, Natalie's side, was covered with magazines and old newspapers and a paperback folded open and face down on the comforter. Out of habit Natalie took one of the subscription forms from a magazine and used it to mark Annie's place.

Normally she would have straightened the covers, neatly stacked the magazines, but under the circumstances felt she lacked the authority to do that. Though the most familiar room, even here something was different.

She was back in the living room before she realized what was missing. Annie had removed all pictures of Natalie from the walls and desk tops, bookcases and counters. She wondered if her presence was that easily exorcised.

Natalie sat in her living room — or what used to be hers. She looked out the windows at the hill, which appeared safe and secure in the afternoon light. The sun had already left the lower part of the yard, but blazed brilliantly towards the top. She closed her eyes and heard the familiar sounds of the house, as familiar to her as her own breathing, unnoticeable unless she took the time to listen. The humming pulse of the refrigerator, the ticking of the clock above the stove, the brass bell sweetly chiming outside. Even the birds singing.

She was reminded of evenings she'd spent waiting for Annie to come home from a late edit. Sitting in limbo in the dark house until Annie walked in and brought everything to life. Suddenly Natalie would have a reason to turn on the lights, put on some music, bring out all the bright incidents of the day, stories to be shared. Up until the sound of her car in the driveway what had been dark and still suddenly was alive. Suddenly everything had a reason, everything she'd brought home from the market, or the extra care she'd taken to set the table nicely even though they were having leftovers — all would be paid off the moment Annie walked in and said, "The house looks lovely," or, "What beautiful flowers," or just, "Hi, hon." The special care she'd taken with herself — the perfume dabbed not just at her temples and neck but behind her knees, inside her elbows — would be rewarded when they embraced and Annie would say, "Umm, you smell good" and hold her an extra second before letting go.

She thought of all the little occasions they celebrated. The anniversary of the day they met, the first time they slept together, when they moved in. Most important now was the anniversary of their commitment ceremony. That gave them their place on the calendar, superceded all other dates they'd marked.

These were all the things Natalie had forgotten lately, skipped over in her haste to tumble into bed with Maggie. She didn't know if she would have the power to convey to Annie how deeply she felt her new convictions. She didn't even know if Annie would care to hear what they were.

She heard Annie's car in the driveway. She had a moment of suspense — would Annie come in, or just drive away when she saw the Mercedes? The moment stretched to an eternity as Annie's car idled outside the window. What was she thinking? Turn and run, get out while the going's good?

Natalie listened then for each familiar sound — the garage door swinging up, the engine running a few extra seconds before being shut off, the car door opening and closing. Tony raced to the gate to greet Annie. Natalie listened as Annie's steps came up the walk. The sound of Annie's loafers scuffing along, scraping against the stone. Keys jingling now as Annie came to the door.

Natalie's heart was racing, pounding as if it would beat itself out of her chest. Panic, but of a different kind than she'd experienced lately, set in. She'd never been so clear about what she wanted. But it all depended on Annie, who at that moment was entering the house. Natalie ran her hands through her hair, took a deep breath and let it out. Saying a small prayer for the first time in her life, she pushed herself off the couch and went to greet Annie at the door. She could ignore her pounding heart now. Natalie knew she wasn't dying, she was hoping to be re-born.

Chapter Fourteen
Night Flights

Blair fought an instinct to bolt from the airport. This was crazy. She had dropped everything to visit a woman who wouldn't even know she was there. And who, if she did know, would want her to leave. Blair hadn't made a conscious decision to fly up to see her mother. One minute she was standing with Lillian, the next minute hurrying out to her car.

Since her last fight with Constance, Blair had focused on her mother's violent denunciation; she had allowed no nuance to dilute her strong negative memories. Now other incidents came to her, startling in their revelation of a side of her mother she'd deliberately ignored. Until now, she hadn't let herself remember back past her father's death.

As the plane hurtled down the runway and lunged up into the darkness, those other times rushed towards Blair, little bright notes of memory that pelted her in no chronological order — being led through museum galleries closed to the public, no one there but her mother and the other docents; being introduced to patients and doctors at the hospital where her mother volunteered. Constance had seemed so interested in everything, so open. How could Blair have forgotten?

But then she'd had reason to make herself forget those times when she'd been proud of her mother. Three years ago Blair would have done anything — short of denying who she was — to make her mother happy. Logic and reason, even the literature she sent Constance, had fallen on a closed mind. Nothing could make Constance understand or accept her daughter. Some part of Blair couldn't, or wouldn't, forgive her mother for shutting her out.

The plane hummed smoothly up the coast towards San Francisco, travelling with a full moon that lit a lake of clouds. Blair looked down at the unopened magazine in her lap. The thought of actually seeing her mother jolted her and she uttered a short involuntary gasp.

• • • • •

This wasn't her mother. Blair was certain of that. The woman tied to the bed by tubes in her arm and nose was drawn and gaunt, the skin around her nose and cheeks pinched and jaundiced, waxy in the fluorescent glow from the light behind her bed. Blair didn't know where her real mother was, but knew she wasn't lying in this hospital bed.

She couldn't bring herself to sit down.

The night nurse came in. "Are you her daughter?" she asked efficiently. Blair nodded tentatively. "We're still monitoring her every half hour," the nurse said, checking her patient's pulse. She pulled back the eyelids and shone her flashlight on the pupils. Took the patient's blood pressure. Checked the IV's, nasal prongs, catheter. Emptied the catheter bag and measured the contents, "So we know how much fluid to give your mother to keep her kidneys functioning properly."

Quit calling her my mother.

The nurse did everything efficiently. After she left, taking with her the bustle of activity, the room went flat again.

After a few minutes in which she just stood there, Blair backed out into the corridor. She hadn't said anything to the woman lying in the bed. Hadn't touched her, not even to check to see if she was real, this woman who bore no resemblance to her mother.

Paul was waiting for her in the lobby. They drove in silence back to his house.

"I'm perfectly fine staying in a hotel," Blair said. Even preferred it, but didn't say that.

"Nonsense," said Paul. "Your room's all ready."

Susan greeted them at the door, smiling when she saw the stuffed bear and the tiger Blair had bought at the airport. "You spoil them, Blair."

"I thought that's what aunts were supposed to do," Blair said, accepting Susan's hug, lingering in her arms an extra moment. "Are my nieces in bed already?"

"Hours ago. It's ten o'clock."

"I guess I lost track of time."

Leaving her luggage in the hall, they trooped into the kitchen. Paul fixed sandwiches for them all. "Who wants beer?" Susan asked.

"Got anything stronger?" Blair requested.

Susan suddenly stood still. "Did you hear that?"

"What?" Blair asked.

"The baby," Susan said. "I'll be right back. Don't wait." She went up the back stairs.

"She's got a mother's ears," Paul said. "We'll be sound asleep and she can hear if one of them so much as coughs." He indicated the cabinet over the refrigerator. "I'll join you." Blair took down a bottle of Glenlivet and poured each of them a glass.

She was afraid her sister-in-law wasn't going to come back down. Susan had muttered something like "Give you two a chance to talk." The last thing in the world Blair was up for. She and Paul went into the living room.

Collapsed in a chair across the coffee table from her brother, Blair swirled the ice in her drink, ignoring her sandwich. She looked around the comfortable room, admiring the warm environment Susan had created. "Susan's got good taste."

"I picked out everything in this room," Paul said.

"You didn't."

"Really. Susan was busy with work and I couldn't stand the empty room any more."

"Maybe you should consider switching careers. You could market yourself as probably the only straight interior designer in the Bay Area."

"Jesus, does everything have to be gay with you?" Paul snapped.

"I was just making a joke."

They sat in strained silence. Blair took a bite of her sandwich, but the food stuck in her throat. She pushed it down with a swallow of her drink. "Look, I didn't come up here to fight with you."

"Why did you come, by the way? Don't you think you're a little late?"

Stung, Blair had to admit: "Maybe."

Paul snorted. "Yeah, maybe." He had sunk down, head against the back of the couch. He looked as exhausted as she felt.

She wanted to apologize for something; not for her decorating quip, but for the past. "You did the best you could, Paul."

His defenses were down. He started to cry, just sat there and cried in front of her, not even bothering to shield his eyes or wipe away the tears. "It was the hardest thing I ever had to do. We just couldn't manage her here. But that place scared her, I think. She was so disoriented, and she got worse real fast." Without looking up at Blair, he said, "I should have done something sooner, like you said."

"It wouldn't have made a difference. You did the right thing."

"When she was okay, she was so . . ." He groped for the word, "Adamant about what she wanted and didn't want."

"Tell me about it." Blair smiled. Paul also managed a weak grin.

"She wasn't herself for such a long time I've almost forgotten how she used to be," he said.

"Difficult," Blair said, hoping he would pick up on the humor in her tone. He did.

"Remember the week of silence?" Paul asked.

"I haven't thought about that in years," Blair said. Constance hadn't talked to her husband for a solid week, wouldn't even speak to the children if he was present.

Paul was shaking his head. "He must have done something really awful that time."

"Probably a more serious affair than usual," Blair ventured. She had never talked about this with her brother.

"That's what I thought." Paul sipped his drink. So they'd both known what was going on, even if they'd never discussed it. "I vowed I'd never be like that," Paul continued. "I guess I take after Mom in that area."

Well, we know who I favor, Blair thought.

"I'll never understand why she didn't leave him."

They talked tentatively about things they remembered, old jealousies and private jokes. For the first time Blair looked at Paul as an individual, not a relative. For the first time she saw something that she liked about this stubborn, gentle man sitting across from her, this brother she hardly knew.

• • • • •

Paul was making hot cereal when Blair came down the next morning. Susan was getting the baby dressed. Little Connie was delighted to find Aunt Blair at the breakfast table and expressed her delight by hiding behind the butcher block island in the middle of the room, peeking out with a loud "Boo!" before running to the huge bear sitting at her place. It took her a few minutes before she could directly acknowledge Blair's presence, but when her initial shyness dissipated she clambered onto Blair's lap to give her a sweet little kiss on the cheek.

Susan came in carrying Alexandra, who had grown amazingly. "She's beautiful," Blair exclaimed, and she was. Huge violet eyes, a big round face.

Susan was off to a meeting. She listed last-minute instructions to Paul, who knew everything already, and said hasty good-byes.

Blair didn't push herself on this niece she hardly knew, merely watched how good Paul was with her. He accepted every soggy banana she fed him with her sticky fingers, letting her play with his moustache as he spooned the last few bites of cereal into her mouth. How had he learned to be so gentle with his children? Certainly not from their father.

After Alexandra finished eating she demanded to be let out of her high chair. She lumbered around the kitchen, chasing after the cat. She was a very good-natured baby, always chirping out great gasps of delight at some discovery she made — the stainless steel band on Blair's watch was a particularly good find, rivaled only by her father's leg.

Blair had never been good at recognizing parents

in the faces of their babies, but this morning she had one very clear moment of looking at Alexandra and seeing not just Susan and Paul, but Constance and Andrew and their parents, her grandparents, and could only assume also generations of both sides of the family. A strong sense of lots of people behind that little face with the round eyes. And continuity. *Paul's family,* she thought. Where had he learned to do this?

The doctor didn't offer Blair and Paul much hope. "About the only thing we can do is keep her stable and as comfortable as possible."

"I want you to do everything you can," Paul insisted.

"That isn't much at this point."

This wasn't enough for Paul, who kept arguing for more aggressive measures. Blair watched him battle for the impossible, wanted to tell him it didn't matter what they did. She stayed out of it, though, feeling she had no claim to a voice under the circumstances.

Afterward, Paul was exhausted. All the relief he'd been given from spending time with his children had been used up. He gave Blair an awkward peck on the cheek before leaving for work. "I'll see you back at the house tonight." The elevator door closed between them.

Blair went down the hall to her mother's room. She sat in the chair at the foot of the bed. An attendant came in and dumped the trash — there wasn't much. Mom isn't much of a consumer these days, Blair wanted to joke, immediately censuring herself. You're sick, Wilder.

A different nurse came in. "Are you her daughter?"

Again Blair nodded. Again the woman was all efficiency, checking the same things the night nurse had, repositioning Constance on the bed. "Some people believe she can hear you, so you might want to talk to your mother."

The burden of those words hung on Blair for almost an hour as she sat in the uncomfortable chair at the foot of the bed, her head full of an accumulation of dreams and reality, snippets of conversation and odd bits of information. Had someone been there to ask what she was thinking, she would have said "Nothing," because there was just too much to choose from.

But someone was there. Labored breathing from the woman in the bed, a rhythm Blair had grown accustomed to, reminded her that someone else was in the room.

You might want to talk to your mother.

How could she be sure this was her mother? Or even the woman who used to be her mother.

Say something to your mother.

Shot back to the past, hearing that gentle coaxing from Constance. *"What do you say, Blair?"* *"Thank you."* *"Good girl."*

Say something to your mother.

But what? It had been so long since she'd relied on her mother for anything that she sat mute, driven deeper into her thoughts.

Some of her friends talked to their mothers. Got and gave advice, went shopping, visited every so often. Her friends blamed, thanked, consulted, borrowed from or supported, listened to, complained about, received gifts from, sent presents to, admired, respected, laughed with and sometimes fondly at, their mothers.

Blair hadn't discussed a book, play, movie, career or home buying decision with her mother in years. Hadn't told her about women she'd dated, flirted with, become friends with.

Hadn't visited, been visited by, gotten a phone call or message from her mother. Not a card. Not a line. Not a word. She couldn't say her mother was her best friend. Not even an acquaintance.

"Where were you?" she began quietly from her chair. "I needed you."

Inside, loudly, furiously, she railed against her mother. "What you did wasn't right and now it's too late for us." Blair didn't think the small room could contain her rage and fury. All the wasted time! She was ashamed of herself for doing this now, with her mother in this condition. Still, she didn't stop. "I didn't become who I am to hurt you. How could you not understand that!"

Blair pulled her chair to her mother's side. For the first time she touched the woman in the bed, reaching her hand out slowly to smooth away the hair matted on her forehead. She sat quietly for a moment before leaning forward to stroke her mother's arm. She talked quietly and steadily into her mother's ear now, no longer angry. Where were her tears? Had she shed them all that night with Roxanne, and the subsequent nights of her dreams? As she maintained her rhythmic stroking, she explained herself to her mother, told her mother what she had never articulated. She apologized to her mother then, not for being who she was, because she was fiercely proud of that, but for not trying harder — or sooner — to bring about a reconciliation between them. She told her mother about all her dreams, their visits, and hoped they would continue.

You might want to talk to your mother.

Yes, Blair wanted to talk to Constance. Nothing could stop her now.

When Blair said, "I love you," she believed Constance heard her, because her breathing changed slightly, and the movement behind her closed lids stopped, just for that moment.

When she had finished talking, Blair went into the bathroom and wet a washcloth, wrung it out over the sink. She brought it to the bedside, and gently wiped her mother's face with it.

Blair stayed at Paul's house another two nights. She spent her days at the hospital with Constance, sometimes sitting quietly, sometimes talking, in a one-sided way making up for lost time. At night she would go home to her nieces, and the warmth of Paul's house.

At dinner the last night, Blair and Paul and Susan discussed Constance's future. Constance's condition required more attention than her nursing home could give her, and her doctor had recommended several chronic care facilities. They made their decisions calmly, without fighting. With a minimum of awkwardness, Blair said she didn't think there was much point in her staying longer. Paul and Susan agreed. "I can be back at a moment's notice."

At the airport, Paul didn't drive off. He pulled the emergency brake, got out, came around to her and gave her a big hug.

Blair couldn't remember the last time they had touched. "Go home. Get some rest," she said, her voice cracking.

"I will," he said.

Blair followed the car with blurred vision until it pulled out of sight.

The plane dipped almost imperceptibly. They must have begun their descent. Blair peered out the window, but it was still too early to see any landmarks she'd recognize.

Something had made her call Roxanne from the hospital earlier that day and explain where she was and why she was there. Roxanne was going to be waiting for her at LAX. Blair had said no, don't bother, but Roxanne had insisted.

"And don't worry," Roxanne added, "It doesn't have to *mean* anything."

Thought Blair, Maybe it might be all right if it did.

244

A few of the publications of
THE NAIAD PRESS, INC.
P.O. Box 10543 ● Tallahassee, Florida 32302
Phone (904) 539-5965
Mail orders welcome. Please include 15% postage.

A ROOM FULL OF WOMEN by Elisabeth Nonas. 256 pp.
Contemporary Lesbian lives.　　　　　ISBN 0-941483-69-X　　$8.95

MURDER IS RELATIVE by Karen Saum. 256 pp. The first
Brigid Donovan mystery.　　　　　ISBN 0-941483-70-3　　8.95

PRIORITIES by Lynda Lyons 288 pp. Science fiction with a
twist.　　　　　ISBN 0-941483-66-5　　8.95

THEME FOR DIVERSE INSTRUMENTS by Jane Rule.
208 pp. Powerful romantic lesbian stories.　ISBN 0-941483-63-0　　8.95

LESBIAN QUERIES by Hertz & Ertman. 112 pp. The questions
you were too embarrassed to ask.　　　ISBN 0-941483-67-3　　8.95

CLUB 12 by Amanda Kyle Williams. 288 pp. Espionage thriller
featuring a lesbian agent!　　　　　ISBN 0-941483-64-9　　8.95

DEATH DOWN UNDER by Claire McNab. 240 pp. 3rd Det.
Insp. Carol Ashton mystery.　　　　ISBN 0-941483-39-8　　8.95

MONTANA FEATHERS by Penny Hayes. 256 pp. Vivian and
Elizabeth find love in frontier Montana.　ISBN 0-941483-61-4　　8.95

CHESAPEAKE PROJECT by Phyllis Horn. 304 pp. Jessie &
Meredith in perilous adventure.　　　ISBN 0-941483-58-4　　8.95

LIFESTYLES by Jackie Calhoun. 224 pp. Contemporary Lesbian
lives and loves.　　　　　ISBN 0-941483-57-6　　8.95

VIRAGO by Karen Marie Christa Minns. 208 pp. Darsen has
chosen Ginny.　　　　　ISBN 0-941483-56-8　　8.95

WILDERNESS TREK by Dorothy Tell. 192 pp. Six women on
vacation learning "new" skills.　　　ISBN 0-941483-60-6　　8.95

MURDER BY THE BOOK by Pat Welch. 256 pp. A Helen
Black Mystery. First in a series.　　　ISBN 0-941483-59-2　　8.95

BERRIGAN by Vicki P. McConnell. 176 pp. Youthful Lesbian–
romantic, idealistic Berrigan.　　　ISBN 0-941483-55-X　　8.95

LESBIANS IN GERMANY by Lillian Faderman & B. Eriksson.
128 pp. Fiction, poetry, essays.　　　ISBN 0-941483-62-2　　8.95

THE BEVERLY MALIBU by Katherine V. Forrest. 288 pp. A
Kate Delafield Mystery. 3rd in a series.　ISBN 0-941483-47-9　　16.95

THERE'S SOMETHING I'VE BEEN MEANING TO TELL
YOU Ed. by Loralee MacPike. 288 pp. Gay men and lesbians
coming out to their children.　　　ISBN 0-941483-44-4　　9.95
　　　　　ISBN 0-941483-54-1　　16.95

LIFTING BELLY by Gertrude Stein. Ed. by Rebecca Mark. 104
pp. Erotic poetry.   ISBN 0-941483-51-7   8.95
                                                      ISBN 0-941483-53-3   14.95

ROSE PENSKI by Roz Perry. 192 pp. Adult lovers in a long-term
relationship.   ISBN 0-941483-37-1   8.95

AFTER THE FIRE by Jane Rule. 256 pp. Warm, human novel
by this incomparable author.   ISBN 0-941483-45-2   8.95

SUE SLATE, PRIVATE EYE by Lee Lynch. 176 pp. The gay
folk of Peacock Alley are *all* cats.   ISBN 0-941483-52-5   8.95

CHRIS by Randy Salem. 224 pp. Golden oldie. Handsome Chris
and her adventures.   ISBN 0-941483-42-8   8.95

THREE WOMEN by March Hastings. 232 pp. Golden oldie. A
triangle among wealthy sophisticates.   ISBN 0-941483-43-6   8.95

RICE AND BEANS by Valeria Taylor. 232 pp. Love and
romance on poverty row.   ISBN 0-941483-41-X   8.95

PLEASURES by Robbi Sommers. 204 pp. Unprecedented
eroticism.   ISBN 0-941483-49-5   8.95

EDGEWISE by Camarin Grae. 372 pp. Spellbinding
adventure.   ISBN 0-941483-19-3   9.95

FATAL REUNION by Claire McNab. 216 pp. 2nd Det. Inspec.
Carol Ashton mystery.   ISBN 0-941483-40-1   8.95

KEEP TO ME STRANGER by Sarah Aldridge. 372 pp. Romance
set in a department store dynasty.   ISBN 0-941483-38-X   9.95

HEARTSCAPE by Sue Gambill. 204 pp. American lesbian in
Portugal.   ISBN 0-941483-33-9   8.95

IN THE BLOOD by Lauren Wright Douglas. 252 pp. Lesbian
science fiction adventure fantasy   ISBN 0-941483-22-3   8.95

THE BEE'S KISS by Shirley Verel. 216 pp. Delicate, delicious
romance.   ISBN 0-941483-36-3   8.95

RAGING MOTHER MOUNTAIN by Pat Emmerson. 264 pp.
Furosa Firechild's adventures in Wonderland. ISBN 0-941483-35-5   8.95

IN EVERY PORT by Karin Kallmaker. 228 pp. Jessica's sexy,
adventuresome travels.   ISBN 0-941483-37-7   8.95

OF LOVE AND GLORY by Evelyn Kennedy. 192 pp. Exciting
WWII romance.   ISBN 0-941483-32-0   8.95

CLICKING STONES by Nancy Tyler Glenn. 288 pp. Love
transcending time.   ISBN 0-941483-31-2   8.95

SURVIVING SISTERS by Gail Pass. 252 pp. Powerful love
story.   ISBN 0-941483-16-9   8.95

SOUTH OF THE LINE by Catherine Ennis. 216 pp. Civil War
adventure.   ISBN 0-941483-29-0   8.95

WOMAN PLUS WOMAN by Dolores Klaich. 300 pp. Supurb
Lesbian overview.   ISBN 0-941483-28-2   9.95

SLOW DANCING AT MISS POLLY'S by Sheila Ortiz Taylor.
96 pp. Lesbian Poetry   ISBN 0-941483-30-4   7.95

DOUBLE DAUGHTER by Vicki P. McConnell. 216 pp. A Nyla
Wade Mystery, third in the series.   ISBN 0-941483-26-6   8.95

HEAVY GILT by Delores Klaich. 192 pp. Lesbian detective/
disappearing homophobes/upper class gay society.

                                       ISBN 0-941483-25-8   8.95

THE FINER GRAIN by Denise Ohio. 216 pp. Brilliant young
college lesbian novel.   ISBN 0-941483-11-8   8.95

THE AMAZON TRAIL by Lee Lynch. 216 pp. Life, travel & lore
of famous lesbian author.   ISBN 0-941483-27-4   8.95

HIGH CONTRAST by Jessie Lattimore. 264 pp. Women of the
Crystal Palace.   ISBN 0-941483-17-7   8.95

OCTOBER OBSESSION by Meredith More. Josie's rich, secret
Lesbian life.   ISBN 0-941483-18-5   8.95

LESBIAN CROSSROADS by Ruth Baetz. 276 pp. Contemporary
Lesbian lives.   ISBN 0-941483-21-5   9.95

BEFORE STONEWALL: THE MAKING OF A GAY AND
LESBIAN COMMUNITY by Andrea Weiss & Greta Schiller.
96 pp., 25 illus.   ISBN 0-941483-20-7   7.95

WE WALK THE BACK OF THE TIGER by Patricia A. Murphy.
192 pp. Romantic Lesbian novel/beginning women's movement.

                                       ISBN 0-941483-13-4   8.95

SUNDAY'S CHILD by Joyce Bright. 216 pp. Lesbian athletics, at
last the novel about sports.   ISBN 0-941483-12-6   8.95

OSTEN'S BAY by Zenobia N. Vole. 204 pp. Sizzling adventure
romance set on Bonaire.   ISBN 0-941483-15-0   8.95

LESSONS IN MURDER by Claire McNab. 216 pp. 1st Det. Inspec.
Carol Ashton mystery — erotic tension!. ISBN 0-941483-14-2   8.95

YELLOWTHROAT by Penny Hayes. 240 pp. Margarita, bandit,
kidnaps Julia.   ISBN 0-941483-10-X   8.95

SAPPHISTRY: THE BOOK OF LESBIAN SEXUALITY by
Pat Califia. 3d edition, revised. 208 pp.   ISBN 0-941483-24-X 8.95

CHERISHED LOVE by Evelyn Kennedy. 192 pp. Erotic
Lesbian love story.   ISBN 0-941483-08-8   8.95

LAST SEPTEMBER by Helen R. Hull. 208 pp. Six stories & a
glorious novella.   ISBN 0-941483-09-6   8.95

THE SECRET IN THE BIRD by Camarin Grae. 312 pp. Striking,
psychological suspense novel.   ISBN 0-941483-05-3   8.95

TO THE LIGHTNING by Catherine Ennis. 208 pp. Romantic Lesbian 'Robinson Crusoe' adventure. ISBN 0-941483-06-1   8.95

THE OTHER SIDE OF VENUS by Shirley Verel. 224 pp. Luminous, romantic love story. ISBN 0-941483-07-X   8.95

DREAMS AND SWORDS by Katherine V. Forrest. 192 pp. Romantic, erotic, imaginative stories. ISBN 0-941483-03-7   8.95

MEMORY BOARD by Jane Rule. 336 pp. Memorable novel about an aging Lesbian couple. ISBN 0-941483-02-9   9.95

THE ALWAYS ANONYMOUS BEAST by Lauren Wright Douglas. 224 pp. A Caitlin Reese mystery. First in a series. ISBN 0-941483-04-5   8.95

SEARCHING FOR SPRING by Patricia A. Murphy. 224 pp. Novel about the recovery of love. ISBN 0-941483-00-2   8.95

DUSTY'S QUEEN OF HEARTS DINER by Lee Lynch. 240 pp. Romantic blue-collar novel. ISBN 0-941483-01-0   8.95

PARENTS MATTER by Ann Muller. 240 pp. Parents' relationships with Lesbian daughters and gay sons. ISBN 0-930044-91-6   9.95

THE PEARLS by Shelley Smith. 176 pp. Passion and fun in the Caribbean sun. ISBN 0-930044-93-2   7.95

MAGDALENA by Sarah Aldridge. 352 pp. Epic Lesbian novel set on three continents. ISBN 0-930044-99-1   8.95

THE BLACK AND WHITE OF IT by Ann Allen Shockley. 144 pp. Short stories. ISBN 0-930044-96-7   7.95

SAY JESUS AND COME TO ME by Ann Allen Shockley. 288 pp. Contemporary romance. ISBN 0-930044-98-3   8.95

LOVING HER by Ann Allen Shockley. 192 pp. Romantic love story. ISBN 0-930044-97-5   7.95

MURDER AT THE NIGHTWOOD BAR by Katherine V. Forrest. 240 pp. A Kate Delafield mystery. Second in a series. ISBN 0-930044-92-4   8.95

ZOE'S BOOK by Gail Pass. 224 pp. Passionate, obsessive love story. ISBN 0-930044-95-9   7.95

WINGED DANCER by Camarin Grae. 228 pp. Erotic Lesbian adventure story. ISBN 0-930044-88-6   8.95

PAZ by Camarin Grae. 336 pp. Romantic Lesbian adventurer with the power to change the world. ISBN 0-930044-89-4   8.95

SOUL SNATCHER by Camarin Grae. 224 pp. A puzzle, an adventure, a mystery — Lesbian romance. ISBN 0-930044-90-8   8.95

THE LOVE OF GOOD WOMEN by Isabel Miller. 224 pp. Long-awaited new novel by the author of the beloved *Patience and Sarah*. ISBN 0-930044-81-9   8.95

INLAND PASSAGE AND OTHER STORIES by Jane Rule. 288 pp. Wide-ranging new collection. ISBN 0-930044-56-8 7.95

WE TOO ARE DRIFTING by Gale Wilhelm. 128 pp. Timeless Lesbian novel, a masterpiece. ISBN 0-930044-61-4 6.95

AMATEUR CITY by Katherine V. Forrest. 224 pp. A Kate Delafield mystery. First in a series. ISBN 0-930044-55-X 8.95

THE SOPHIE HOROWITZ STORY by Sarah Schulman. 176 pp. Engaging novel of madcap intrigue. ISBN 0-930044-54-1 7.95

THE BURNTON WIDOWS by Vickie P. McConnell. 272 pp. A Nyla Wade mystery, second in the series. ISBN 0-930044-52-5 7.95

OLD DYKE TALES by Lee Lynch. 224 pp. Extraordinary stories of our diverse Lesbian lives. ISBN 0-930044-51-7 8.95

DAUGHTERS OF A CORAL DAWN by Katherine V. Forrest. 240 pp. Novel set in a Lesbian new world. ISBN 0-930044-50-9 8.95

THE PRICE OF SALT by Claire Morgan. 288 pp. A milestone novel, a beloved classic. ISBN 0-930044-49-5 8.95

AGAINST THE SEASON by Jane Rule. 224 pp. Luminous, complex novel of interrelationships. ISBN 0-930044-48-7 8.95

LOVERS IN THE PRESENT AFTERNOON by Kathleen Fleming. 288 pp. A novel about recovery and growth.
ISBN 0-930044-46-0 8.95

TOOTHPICK HOUSE by Lee Lynch. 264 pp. Love between two Lesbians of different classes. ISBN 0-930044-45-2 7.95

MADAME AURORA by Sarah Aldridge. 256 pp. Historical novel featuring a charismatic "seer." ISBN 0-930044-44-4 7.95

CURIOUS WINE by Katherine V. Forrest. 176 pp. Passionate Lesbian love story, a best-seller. ISBN 0-930044-43-6 8.95

BLACK LESBIAN IN WHITE AMERICA by Anita Cornwell. 141 pp. Stories, essays, autobiography. ISBN 0-930044-41-X 7.95

CONTRACT WITH THE WORLD by Jane Rule. 340 pp. Powerful, panoramic novel of gay life. ISBN 0-930044-28-2 9.95

MRS. PORTER'S LETTER by Vicki P. McConnell. 224 pp. The first Nyla Wade mystery. ISBN 0-930044-29-0 7.95

These are just a few of the many Naiad Press titles — we are the oldest and largest lesbian/feminist publishing company in the world. Please request a complete catalog. We offer personal service; we encourage and welcome direct mail orders from individuals who have limited access to bookstores carrying our publications.